THE MYSTERY OF THE EXISTENTIAL ENVOY

THE THREE INVESTIGATORS

IN

THE MYSTERY OF THE EXISTENTIAL ENVOY

BY

ELIZABETH ARTHUR
& STEVEN BAUER

BASED ON CHARACTERS
CREATED BY ROBERT ARTHUR

Hollow Tree Press 2025

CONTENTS

1

A Confrontation With Evil

Pete Crenshaw tossed the ball into the air and, as it fell, he swung, hard. The *ping* an ash bat made hitting a hardball right was one of the sweetest sounds in the world, and from the vibration he felt in his hands, he knew he'd hit a homer. Or he would have if he'd been playing baseball. The ball shot from the bat and flew straight into the batting cage where it hit the nylon net with a whisper and fell to the ground.

It was a sunny Saturday morning at the beginning of August, and although Pete had been planning to go to the Rocky Beach Animal Rescue Center first thing this morning to help out, since he hadn't actually told Mr. Munson when he'd be coming, he'd thought he'd steal a little time for batting practice. However, he was already feeling guilty about his choice.

Not only had he − sort of − broken his word to Mr. Munson, but he'd also − sort of − broken his word to the animals he was taking care of − and since he and his best friends Jupiter Jones and Bob Andrews didn't have a case

7

to investigate at the moment, he didn't have much of an excuse.

Of course, Jupiter had often told him and Bob that you never knew when a case would pop up, and as Pete had walked the six blocks from his house to the small pocket park at the corner of Acacia and Broad, he'd kept an eye out. The Rec Department of the town of Rocky Beach had developed the park several years before. Half the size of a square block, it was a great place to get some exercise or to relax.

There were swings and slides, monkey bars, and a spinner for younger children, two basketball hoops and the batting cage, as well as benches and three picnic tables. Though Pete had arrived early, before it got too hot, already the swings were full. Parents pushed their kids as the children screamed. There was another noise Pete heard, jangly and discordant, as if someone was playing music outside – music Pete didn't like.

Pete picked up another ball from the bucket at his feet, tossed it, and swung again. This time the hit was less solid and it veered off to the right. Darn, Pete thought. He and Bob and Jupiter would be freshmen at Rocky Beach High in the fall, and Pete planned to try out for

the varsity soccer team in the fall and the baseball team in the spring. It would be a change,
moving from softball to baseball, and he
wanted to get a head start. He'd done well on
the junior high softball team, but not as well as
he'd hoped, even if his batting average *had* been
the best.

He picked up another ball, tossed it, and
swung. Ping! Another winner. Pete dropped the
bat and raised his arms into the air. "Go,
Badgers!" he yelled and did a little victory
dance.

"You done?" a voice said behind him.

He turned, embarrassed. He could feel
his face get hot. A younger boy was standing
about ten feet away with a bat and a bucket of
softballs. He was shorter than Pete, with
squinty eyes and scruffy blond hair that peeked
out from under his baseball cap, which he wore
backwards. He was a scrappy kid who Pete
had seen walking his dog, a Golden Retriever,
around the neighborhood. Pete had even spoken to him once or twice.

"You came down to practice your
swing," Pete said, stating the obvious. "You're
Mickie, right?"

"Close," the boy said. "Mikey." He
looked pleased that Pete had remembered him.

Pete picked up his bat and rested it on his shoulder. "I'm almost done. I'm Pete," he said.

Mikey nodded as if he knew. "Come on over," Pete said. "Let's see what you can do. What grade are you in? I think I knew but I forgot."

"Seventh, in the fall," Mikey said.

"Go on," Pete said, gesturing to the cage. "Don't mind me."

But Pete's presence clearly made the younger boy nervous. He tossed a softball up and swung, missing it. He winced, picked it up, and threw it in the air again. This time he got a solid hit. The bigger ball made a thwack and flew into the batting cage's net.

"Good one," Pete said. "That would have been a double, at least!"

A high-pitched earsplitting shriek rent the air, so loud and jarring Pete put his hands to his ears. "Ouch!" he said. "What was that?"

"Existential Evil," Mikey said.

Pete looked at him, baffled. "What?"

"It's a garage band," Mikey said. "That was probably one of their amplifiers. They always practice on Saturday morning, no matter how many people tell them to can it. Kyle Bault and his friends."

"Who's Kyle Bault?" Pete asked.

"He's some guy," Mikey said. "I think he was in prison for a while, but now he's home living with his parents. About a block from my house."

Maybe that noise he'd heard earlier – someone might call it music, he guessed – had been this garage band.

"They're pretty terrible," Pete said.

"Yeah," Mikey agreed. "They just like to rock out."

"Well," said Pete, gesturing toward the cage. "It's all yours, Mikey. I've got to go, anyway. I'm volunteering at the Animal Rescue Center today."

"Really? That's terrific!" Mikey said. "We got our Golden Retriever from them. At the time, they didn't know *what* he was, though. He was really little and covered in mud. The guy who had him chained him up outside."

"I can't understand how anyone can do stuff like that," Pete said.

"Me, neither," said Mikey. "Did you hear about that guy they arrested down in San Diego? The one with the parrots?"

Pete shook his head. Mikey suddenly looked angry.

"It was in the paper," he said. "They

caught him trying to smuggle some sort of little parrots into the country from South America. They were blue and he'd stuffed them inside blue plastic hair curlers. They couldn't move or make any noise. When the Customs guys found them, they were almost starved to death. A bunch of them had already died."

The thought of it made Pete's stomach lurch. "That's awful," he said.

"My dad said he thought some bird shop in Rocky Beach might be bringing parrots into the country illegally."

"Why does he think that?" Pete asked. "What bird shop?"

"I don't know. It's a woman's name. V something," Mikey said. "He heard some rumor, I guess."

Pete was already feeling upset about the parrots, as well as guilty that he wasn't at the Rescue Center right now, when suddenly the music from the garage band jumped in volume. For the first time, Pete could understand some of the words that they were singing, and they shocked him.

"Did you hear what I just heard?" he asked Mikey.

"Yeah," Mikey said. "It's not the first time."

"But there are little kids here!" Pete said. He suddenly felt truly angry. He might not be able to do anything about the trade in South American parrots, but he could certainly do something about this so-called band playing so close to a playground. "You know these guys?" he asked.

"Just a little," Mikey said. "I'll go with you if you want."

"Let's go," Pete said. He shouldered his bat and picked up his pail of balls. Mikey followed him.

The house was only a few blocks away on Green – the garage door was open and three guys in their late forties or early fifties stood there, whaling on electric guitars. A fourth was beating up a drum set. Pete wasn't sure what "existential" meant, but he thought that "evil" was a pretty good description of the noise the band made.

The lead singer was screaming into a microphone – crass and ugly words that Pete, even at almost fourteen, disliked hearing. The guy was wearing sunglasses, a flowered Hawaiian shirt, a black fedora, and skintight jeans. He was wiry and taut and there was a twang in his voice. His face was hard, with a jaw that jutted forward and looked like it was made of granite.

The guy next to him on bass guitar was medium height, with close-set eyes, olive skin, a shaved head, and several days of stubble. He wore tight black pants and a black muscle shirt. Clearly he lifted weights; his biceps bulged. Around his neck he wore a big gold cross on a substantial gold chain. He looked surly, even a bit threatening.

"The one over there?" Mikey said. "That's Kyle Bault." He pointed to the third guy, the one playing back-up guitar. The drummer had a full beard that looked in danger of catching fire from the cigarette clenched between his teeth.

They played on for a minute, but the lead singer now stared at Pete and Mikey, and when he stopped shouting, the band stopped playing. He took off his fedora and swatted it across his thigh, then strutted out to where the boys stood. Pete could see his hair was thinning, but what was left of it was long and it had been gathered into a bun the hat had hidden.

The man left his sunglasses on, and his eyes were inscrutable. He was taller than Mikey but not taller than Pete. His expression wasn't friendly, but he tried to make his voice hide the way he felt.

"Can I help you?" he asked. "Are you looking for someone?"

"There are very young children right over there," Pete said, pointing toward the playground. "You shouldn't be singing that song so loudly."

By this time, the bass guitarist had joined him. He wrinkled up his nose as if he smelled something unpleasant. "I thought only geezers like your old man gave us trouble," he said to the singer. "What do these kids want?"

"They want us to stop singing so loud," the singer said.

The bald one laughed. "Those kids probably hear worse at home," he said.

"I live right up the block," Mikey said defiantly. "Do you want me to get my dad?"

"Hold on, hold on," the lead singer said. He put his hands out in front of him as if he were trying to stop traffic. "Let's not get carried away. I'm Russell," he said. "And you are?"

"I'm Pete," Pete said. "And this is Mikey."

"Mikey?" the bald guy said, laughing. "Mikey mikey mikey," he chanted in a singsong voice. He was a hothead, Pete saw.

Russell clearly already knew that. "Be

quiet, Slade," he said. To Pete and Mikey he added, "We've got no problem skipping that song for now."

Pete was still trembling with a combination of adrenaline and anger, but they'd done what they'd come to do and he didn't want to hang around another minute. He nudged Mikey who looked up at him with wide eyes. Pete could see he'd been a little scared. So had Pete, but as he and Mikey walked away, he would have been feeling pretty good if it hadn't been for Mikey's story about the parrots.

Pete thanked Mikey for his help and said that he hoped to see him around. Then he headed for home, where he found his mother in the kitchen, making a chicken salad for lunch.

She hummed as she worked – a catchy pop song from a year or two ago. She wore a summer dress with a subdued pattern of tiny roses and looked much younger than she actually was – almost as though she could be Pete's older sister. Her curly black hair cascaded over her shoulders.

When he sat heavily down at the table, still a little shaken, she looked at him appraisingly.

"So what have you been up to?" she asked. Sometimes Pete thought his mother could read his mind. He told her about batting practice and Mikey and Existential Evil.

"You should have heard them," Pete said "They'd have given you a fit. What does 'existential' mean, anyway?"

His mother laughed. "It's one of those big words people use when they're trying to sound really smart," she said. "It refers to existence. For example, if I say that nuclear war is an existential threat, I mean that nuclear war threatens existence. People also use it to talk about big philosophical questions, like how and whether life has meaning, and why human beings exist. Of course it has meaning, and human beings exist to find it!"

She brought him a cup of coffee and sat down across from him. "I actually like the word," she said. "There aren't all that many words in English that remind you of how *interesting* existence really is."

"And not just human existence," said Pete. He'd long been able to confide in his mother, and now he decided to tell her what else was on his mind. He explained about the man arrested in San Diego with the baby parrots and the rumor about a bird shop in Rocky Beach maybe being involved with smuggling.

As he talked, his mother listened carefully, her face a picture of sympathy and understanding. "I thought maybe me, Jupiter, and Bob could look into it," Pete said, "but I'm afraid they might think it's all too vague, or that we should wait for another case to come along."

His mother reached across the table and covered his hand with hers. "First of all," she said, "It's 'Jupiter, Bob, and I.' And second of all, I'm surprised at you! You're not giving your friends enough credit. But I'm interested, too! If you'd like to do a sort of preliminary check on this bird shop, I could take you."

Pete looked at her, surprised. "Really?"

"Of course," his mother said. "Let's find out what it's actually called."

It seemed it was called Veronica's Exotic Birds, and since the shop was just up the block from the Rocky Beach marina, Valeria Crenshaw decided to park in the marina parking lot. The air smelled strongly of salt and the early afternoon sun glinted off the water.

The marina was large, and most of the slips were filled with sailboats, but at the moment there was only one person in sight − a man in his late twenties or early thirties, with skin brown from the sun, and a bristly black mustache. He was wiping down the deck of his sailboat – a good-sized boat with two masts and *Santa María* painted on its hull.

The man looked up as Pete and his mother walked by. "Hey," Pete said cheerily. "That's a beautiful boat."

The man seemed nervous to Pete. "Sí," he said. "Mi inglés es very bod. Muy poco inglés."

"No habla inglés?" Pete said. "Yo hablo español bastante bien. Me llamo Pete."

The man seemed to relax a little at this. "Bueno," he said. "Me llamo José."

As they walked on, Pete's mother congratulated him on how well he was coming along with his Spanish. Although his mother had always spoken fluent Spanish, his father's parents had thought their son should learn only English, so Pete's parents hadn't spoken Spanish together when Pete was a kid.

He and his mother walked side by side as they crossed the parking lot to Veronica's Exotic Birds. A set of bells jangled as Pete pulled open the door, then stepped into a brightly lit store that smelled faintly of wood shavings and something vegetal. In the far back, a young man was emptying a large bag of birdseed into a bright galvanized can. The air was filled with chirping, twittering, and fluttering, punctuated by an occasional birdcall and the sound of a parrot talking to itself.

Pete's eyes immediately landed on a startlingly blue bird with a big curved gray beak sitting calmly on a perch at the front of the store. It was one of the biggest birds Pete had ever seen – about three feet long from the crown of its head to the tip of its tail feathers – and easily the most beautiful. Its feathers were cobalt blue and seemed almost to shimmer with the purity of their blueness. A bright yellow ring surrounded its black eye, and a corresponding yellow stripe accented its bottom beak.

Pete couldn't stop himself. Ignoring everything else, he made a beeline for the bird. It looked even bigger close up. He stood in front of it, awestruck, and the bird looked at him mildly, turning its head to better peer at him. His mother came up behind him.

"This is the most amazing bird I've ever seen!" Pete said to her. "Do you think it's a parrot?"

"Hello," an unfamiliar female voice said. "I'm Veronica Harrison. I see you've already met Agatha."

Pete had been so engrossed admiring the bird that he hadn't noticed the woman walking toward them. She was middle-aged, with short salt and pepper hair and a pleasant face. She'd taken her glasses and perched them on top of her head. She had a name tag that read "Veronica."

She raised her arm and Agatha stepped confidently from her perch to the woman's wrist. She bent her head and the woman scratched her head feathers as she kept talking.

"Hyacinth macaws are native to South America," she said. "They live mostly in a large grassy open wetlands area in Brazil called the Pantanal. They're the largest flying parrots in the world and can live to be fifty or sixty in the wild – even longer in captivity.

"I've had her for fifteen years," she added. "I hand-raised her. She's not for sale, obviously. But a healthy hyacinth macaw can bring $20,000 on the open market these days. Wild ones are very rare – and totally protected. A lot of people wanted them because they're so beautiful, so they were caught and sold as part of the exotic pet trade. And big portions of their habitat have been destroyed as people moved in nearby. I'm very lucky to be able to own a sweetie-pie like this one. She's only here two days a week. At home I have an aviary for her."

"Does she bite?" Pete asked.

The woman smiled. "The beak is for cracking nuts," she said. "In the wild she would eat Brazil nuts."

Just then, the bells on the front door jingled, and Pete turned to see a man entering the shop. He was over six feet tall and in his mid-to-late-40s, Pete thought. His skin was bronze from the sun, his face open and welcoming. He wore a loose-fitting blue tunic over a pair of well-worn jeans and his long jet-black hair was pulled back in a ponytail held with a silver clip.

He carried a largish cage with a bird with a brilliant red head. It was clear at once that he and Veronica knew one another.

"Rafael!" she said. "You're down from Santa Barbara! And you have a scarlet macaw!"

"Temporarily," Rafael said. "I bought him this morning at the Farmer's Market. A Mexican man was selling him for much less than he's worth. The man had no papers showing where the bird came from, and I was worried he was so cheap that someone who wouldn't be able to take care of him properly would buy him on a whim. You don't expect to find endangered birds for sale next to the tomatoes, but there he was."

There was a clatter from the back of the shop, and all four of them turned to look. The young man who'd been filling the can with birdseed looked startled and vaguely guilty. Pete thought he probably always looked guilty.

"Is everything all right, Jack?" the woman asked.

"Yeah," the man said. "I just knocked over a cage." He was in his twenties, with blond hair, a weak chin, and twitchy eyes. Under his lower lip he sprouted a tuft of hair that Pete thought was called a "soul patch." Pete knew it was meant to look hip, but in this case it didn't much work.

The man named Rafael turned back to Veronica. "His name is Rojo," he told her, "and I have nowhere to keep him at the moment. Do you think you could look after him until I leave for Santa Barbara?"

"Of course I could," said Veronica. "But I have to wonder how this Mexican man came to be selling a scarlet macaw in a farmer's market."

Pete had been wondering the same thing, but when Veronica asked her question, his last tinge of suspicion that she herself might be involved in the illegal animal trade vanished. Between the way she'd talked about Agatha and what she'd just said to Rafael, she was clearly one of the good guys. The rumor Mikey's father had heard must have had no basis in fact.

"I wonder, too," said Rafael "And I wish I could think of how to conduct an investigation into the matter."

"Excuse a mother's pride," Valeria Crenshaw said suddenly, "but my son is one of The Three Investigators. Perhaps you've heard of them? They ask a lot of questions, and they investigate anything."

Veronica shook her head, but an expression of interest crossed Rafael's face. "The Three Investigators?" he said.

"You may remember reading in the paper about the three boys who discovered the hidden gold up in Auburn?" Pete's mother said.

"That's it!" Rafael exclaimed. "By the way, my name is Rafael Solares." He reached out to shake Pete's mother's hand, and afterward, Pete's. His grip was warm and powerful.

"I'm Pete Crenshaw," Pete said.

His mother nudged him. "Why don't you give him your card?"

It was a radical idea. Pete did have some Three Investigators' business cards in his wallet, but it had always been Jupiter who handed them out. "Go on," his mother said.

Why not? Pete thought. Why carry them if not for moments like this? He took one out and handed it to Rafael Solares, who glanced at it with interest.

"It's good to meet you, Pete," he said. "I've got a son about your age. You remind me of him a little. He lives with his mother south of San Diego and just north of Tijuana, in Chula Vista."

"Gosh," said Pete. "That's a long way from Santa Barbara."

"Too long," Rafael said.

Pete didn't know what to say to this, so he said nothing as Rafael looked at the card again. It said, as it always had,

THE THREE INVESTIGATORS
"We Investigate Anything"
???
First Investigator – Jupiter Jones
Second Investigator – Pete Crenshaw
Records and Research – Bob Andrews

and at the bottom was the number of the landline in Headquarters, the number of Bob Andrews' cellphone, and the website address of their firm.

Rafael looked up at Pete again. "So you're the Second Investigator," he said. "Well, if you and your friends really investigate anything, maybe I *will* ask you to see what you can find out about Rojo and the man I bought him from. I've got something I need to do first, but I'll think about it and let you know."

"You see?" Pete's mother said triumphantly. "Nothing ventured, nothing gained."

Rafael smiled, then said he had to be going. Veronica promised she'd take good care of Rojo until Rafael came back for him.

"Mrs. Crenshaw," Rafael said, nodding politely. And then he was out of the store and striding toward a battered pickup hand-painted a cheerful bright yellow and parked right outside the shop. Figures that looked like wheels with spokes decorated the doors and tailgate; some had the points of stars radiating from them. A representation of a human figure had been painted with contrasting stripes of black and white – with a single red line down its middle.

The paintings weren't finely drawn, but they were compelling. On the truck's back, a handmade plywood truck cap rose to a gentle point, like the roof of a house. It, too, had been painted with symbols.

"Look at that," said Pete's mother. "Those are Chumash Indian symbols. They look at lot like wall paintings in Chumash Painted Cave State Park! I took my class there just this year."

"Rafael is half-Chumash," Veronica said. "The Chumash originally lived around Los Angeles and Santa Monica, but now they have a reservation up in Santa Ynez, about two hours north of here. About a year ago Rafael was asked to be a sort of Chumash envoy for the Santa Barbara County school system. Now, how can I help you?"

Pete didn't know what to say. They'd come to the store because he'd been suspicious that it was engaged in parrot smuggling. But between Rafael Solares and Veronica Harrison, he now knew his suspicions were misplaced.

"We – we just wanted to look around," Pete said weakly.

His mother, however, seemed fully energized by the challenge of covering up their original purpose. "I'd actually like to buy my son a bird," she said.

Pete's mouth fell open and he looked at her, amazed. "He's always wanted a pet," she explained to Veronica. "A dog would probably be better, but my husband's in the movies and he's away a lot – anyway, I think a bird would be a lovely pet. Do you have any recommendations? Nothing too big, or too hard to take care of," she added.

Veronica smiled. "I have just the thing," she said. She took them to look at the Fischer's lovebirds. They were small parrots, under six inches long, and beautiful. They were very social and did better in pairs, she said. They were found in Tanzania, in Africa, she added. Pete really liked them, but he felt compelled to ask.

"Where do you get your birds?" he said.

"All our birds are bred and born and hand-raised right here in southern California," Veronica said.

All right then, Pete thought.

"We'll take them," Pete's mother said, "and of course a cage and feed and – and whatever they need. Pete works at the Animal Rescue Center so he'll know how to take excellent care."

"Well, good for you, Pete," Veronica said. "I wish more young people took an active interest in animal welfare."

Pete almost said something about the smuggling he was concerned with, but then thought better of it. Jupiter was always saying it was wiser to gather information than to divulge it.

Suddenly, the scarlet macaw, whose cage was now sitting on the counter, started to make noises – first a whooshing sound like wind or water, then a long-drawn-out creaking, and finally, something that sounded to Pete a bit like the engine of a pull-cord lawnmower sputtering before it finally caught.

"Good heavens," said Pete's mother.

She and Pete were even more surprised when Rojo suddenly spoke in a clear voice. "More copy borrows on the way," he said. He hopped on his perch and turned his head to stare at Pete.

"Whoa!" Pete said. "What does that mean?"

"I may be wrong," Ms. Harrison said, "but I think what he's actually saying is 'capybara.'" She shook her head. "I have no idea where on earth he would have learned to say that – or to make those peculiar noises, either!"

"What's a capybara?" Pete asked.

"It's a semi-aquatic South American rodent – like a gigantic guinea pig that loves water," Veronica said. "They can grow to weigh a hundred and forty pounds."

Pete tried to picture the animal. A hundred and forty pound guinea pig?

Still, as he left the store, what Pete was really wondering was what an envoy was. It was cool that the guy he'd just given a Three Investigators card to *was* one, but although he had a vague idea that the word meant something like "ambassador," he really wasn't sure.

"Veronica said that guy is a Chumash envoy to the Santa Barbara County schools," he said, as he and his mother headed for the car. "Can you remind me what an envoy is, exactly?" Pete asked.

His mother looked at him sideways, smiling fondly.

"Just someone from one country who represents it to another one," she said, rooting around in her purse for the keys to the car. "Someone who embodies what the people of his country stand for, and who stands in for them, somehow. Like when the first Queen Elizabeth sent Francis Drake to South America. He was her envoy."

"I get it," said Pete. "Thanks, Mom."

As Pete settled the birdcage with the lovebirds in the back of his mother's car, he had a funny thought. Although the lovebirds had been raised in southern California, since their forebears had been born in Tanzania, maybe you could say that they were envoys for that country. After all, in a way, animals were *always* envoys for the countries they'd come from, he thought.

After he and his mother took the lovebirds home and settled them in, he'd need to keep his promise to Mr. Munson, but this evening he'd give Jupiter a call to tell him about Rafael Solares and the scarlet macaw he'd bought in the Rocky Beach farmer's market. He really felt there was a mystery here somewhere − and one it might be important to investigate!

2

Suspicious Characters

The following day, just after noon, Jupiter was waiting at the Salvage Yard for Pete and Bob to arrive for a Three Investigators meeting and for his Uncle Titus to return from a buying expedition with Leif, one of the Yard's two Norwegian carpenters. Pete had called him the night before to tell him that his mother had bought him two lovebirds at a store called Veronica's Exotic Birds, and that he might have found a mystery for The Three Investigators to look into.

Pete had said only that the mystery involved a bird, so when Uncle Titus and Leif pulled into the Salvage Yard and started unloading his uncle's latest haul, Jupiter was surprised to see that it mostly consisted of cages – bird cages – of bamboo and wicker and metal. He and Magnus pitched in to help unload them, and Aunt Mathilda showed up to supervise. Among the cages were several Victorian beauties with fancy ornamentation as well as some ordinary modern ones.

In a box that Uncle Titus was handing

to Aunt Mathilda, Jupiter was intrigued to see a number of ceramic representations and wooden carvings of birds – all different and all of them hand-painted – and also a carving of a whale that was almost a foot long and seemed to be made from a piece of driftwood. Leif picked it up and held it.

"I like the way it's flipping its tail," he said. "And look at these carved barnacles!"

"That's a humpback," Aunt Mathilda said, taking the carving back from him and placing it firmly in the box.

Just then, both Pete and Bob biked through the wrought-iron gates, and there was a break in the unloading as everyone said hello. Pete looked in the box Aunt Mathilda had just put down.

"Wow, a whale!" he said. He seemed quite surprised to see the cages.

"Gee," he said. "I could have used one of these for my new lovebirds."

Pete filled in Bob, and Leif and Magnus, and Jupiter's aunt and uncle on what Jupiter already knew, then turned to Uncle Titus. "Where did all this stuff come from?" he asked.

"It *is* quite a haul, my boy," said Uncle Titus, "and actually, it's a sad story. This all belonged to a man named Walter Tate – he's

94 years old, if you can believe it, and he fought in the Second World War. He originally taught English at Rocky Beach High School, but he retired a long time ago, and when his wife died six months back, Mr. Tate decided he couldn't keep up with his place any more. He has two children. His daughter asked him to live with her in Sacramento, but he didn't want to move to a city. He and his wife had a rambling old house on two acres up the coast, but now he's moved to an old age home – "

"Titus!" Aunt Mathilda said. "A retirement community!"

Uncle Titus smiled affably. "To a retirement community in Rocky Beach, and his son is selling a lot of stuff, to raise money for the expenses. After all, these old age – "

"Titus!"

"These places cost a lot of spondoolees. Anyway," he went on, "the Tates were bird lovers. There was a huge outdoor aviary as well as all these cages. They had the whole place fenced, as well. They didn't have any normal pets, just birds – and also the darndest thing I ever saw. Three animals that looked like giant guinea pigs! Huge! They were from South America and they liked water. The place has a pond. Capybaras or some such thing."

"Capybaras!" Pete almost shouted.

"Yes!" Uncle Titus said. "They were still there when I bought the cages – waiting to be picked up by a man from Texas. They were kind of cute, actually – big and brown with sloping noses."

Jupiter could see that Pete was dying to ask his uncle questions, but just then his Aunt Mathilda said, "Cold drinks for everyone," and when she returned with lemonade, Jupiter turned to Pete and Bob.

"Come on," he said. "Let's drink this in the workshop. Pete has something he wants to tell us."

The Three Investigators' outdoor workshop was partly shielded from view – positioned not all that far from the truly hidden old mobile home that served as their Headquarters. The boys sat in the green metal chairs they kept there and got down to business.

"So what's all this about a bird?" asked Jupiter. "And why did you look so electrified when my uncle mentioned capybaras?"

"It's sort of a long story," Pete said. "Veronica – who we bought the lovebirds from – is friends with a guy named Rafael Solares who lives up in Isla Vista. I don't know why he's in Rocky Beach, but yesterday morning he bought a scarlet macaw real cheap from a Mexican man at the farmer's market. My mom and I were at Veronica's because a kid I met told me a rumor that Veronica's Exotic Birds might be smuggling South American parrots.

"And?" asked Jupiter.

"Not true," said Pete. "At least I don't think so. But I ended up giving this Rafael Solares our card – when my mother told me to – and he said he might give us a call about a case!"

Jupiter was impressed by how clearly and succinctly Pete had told this story.

"And the capybaras?" he asked.

"Well," said Pete, "after Rafael left the shop, the scarlet macaw – whose name is Rojo – started making really strange noises. One was like a rope creaking, one sounded like a lawnmower, and one was a big whooshing noise. But the weirdest thing was that he said, 'More capybaras on the way.' I'd never even *heard* of capybaras but then I got here and your uncle was talking about them!"

"Wow," Bob said. "That's quite a coincidence."

Hmmm, Jupiter thought. He found himself intrigued by what Pete was reporting. A

Mexican peddler had sold a South American bird for a lot less than it was worth, and it made strange noises. He asked Pete to tell the story again, and this time to take his time and reproduce the noises to the best of his ability. Pete did an admirable job all around; his engine sounded quite authentic as it stumbled into full-throated life, and his creaking and whooshing were excellent.

"Great job, Pete," Bob said. "You could have had a career as an old-time sound effects man."

"Yes, that was excellent, Second," Jupiter said. "Clearly the bird has lived in a place where it heard a wide variety of sounds on a daily basis. Maybe somewhere there were capybaras. What do we know about capybaras? Do you have your laptop with you, Bob?"

Bob nodded and reached for his backpack. He hauled his laptop out and got onto the Salvage Yard's Wi-Fi. After he typed "capybara" in the search engine, he went first to Images, and as Pete and Jupiter crowded around, Jupiter saw that his uncle had been right − capybaras did indeed look like giant guinea pigs. Pete started laughing.

"What?" Bob asked.

"They're like − oh, man," Pete said.

From the online images, capybaras seemed to enjoy carrying other animals on their backs — monkeys, butterflies, and especially birds. Bob pulled up the Wikipedia article and the boys learned that capybaras – found throughout most of South America – were the world's largest rodent. Though they weighed just three pounds at birth, they weighed between 75 and 150 pounds when they were grown.

Also, capybaras were highly social animals who lived in big groups, ate largely grasses, could stay underwater for up to five minutes at a time, and could live to be 10 or 12 years old if they were kept in captivity or as pets. In the wild, they generally lived less than four years, because they were a favorite food of jaguars, pumas, ocelots, eagles, caimans, and anacondas.

"Boy!" said Pete. "With those odds, I bet the capybaras living at that place your uncle went to have been pretty happy!"

"In South America, people sometimes hunt them for their meat and fur," Bob reported, "or because they chow down on grass their cattle eat. But they reproduce really fast and they aren't endangered."

"Look!" Pete said. "It says they can run

as fast as a horse."

"It's not legal to keep them as pets in California, but you can in Pennsylvania and Texas," Bob said. "Which I guess is why that man from Texas is coming to pick them up. What was his name? The guy who taught at Rocky Beach High?"

"Walter Tate," Jupiter said. "My uncle said he lived on two acres with a pond. He'd have to have a pond to keep such aquatic animals. Even so, I'm surprised he had them. Most World War Two veterans and high school English teachers tend to be law-abiding citizens, and although a lot of the rules and regulations the government imposes have no rhyme or reason, 94-year-olds like Walter Tate tend not to break the law if they can help it."

Bob did a little more research. "There's a lot of difference in state law when it comes to keeping exotic pets," he said. " You can own a hedgehog in most states, but not in Pennsylvania or California or Maine or Arizona. In Pennsylvania you can own a wallaby – a sort of mini-kangaroo – if you get a license. And right next door in Ohio you don't even need a license. Maybe Mr. Tate didn't know keeping capybaras was illegal in California."

"That's a good hypothesis, Bob," said

Jupiter. "I wonder why they *are* illegal here?"

Bob did some more research. "It says there's a ban on all non-native wild animals in California, except for birds that have been born in the state and hand-reared. Capybaras are illegal because they could become an invasive species if they escaped into the wild."

Pete chortled. "Yeah, right – with all the wetlands. You know," he added, "if we went out to Walter Tate's place right now, maybe we could see his capybaras before the guy from Texas comes to pick them up."

Bob had just clicked back to the images of capybaras, and Pete added, "Look at that one with a monkey sleeping on his back!"

Jupiter looked at the picture Pete was pointing at and had to agree that it might be interesting to see the actual animal – and since capybaras *were* illegal to keep as pets in California, it might even lead to a case they could investigate. It wasn't likely, but it was possible, he supposed.

"If Aunt Mathilda says yes, maybe Leif or Magnus could drive us back there," Jupiter said.

"Let's go ask!" said Pete.

Jupiter led the way to the office where Aunt Mathilda was now working, and although she hemmed and hawed for a while, eventually she said yes, and since Magnus had finished the carpentry project he'd been working on earlier, he was willing to go for a drive. He consulted with his brother about the best way to get there, then took the wheel of the smaller of the Salvage Yard's trucks.

The drive took about twenty-five minutes – a long drive, Jupiter reflected, for a man who had taught in Rocky Beach for maybe forty-five years. He must have really loved living in the country. Magnus took roads Jupiter had never been on before, and then suddenly they came over the brow of a hill and saw a big Victorian house with a modern deck overlooking a pond.

Even at this distance, Jupiter could see some large brown animals grazing near the water. He had the impression of a tidy and well-loved house and property. As Magnus drove up, Jupiter also saw a panel van parked in front of the house. He asked Magnus to park next to it, but when he and Bob and Pete got out and looked around, they couldn't see anyone it might belong to.

A sign on the lawn said 'Sale Today,' but the sale was clearly over, so Jupiter concluded that the truck must belong to Walter

Tate's son. He'd be in the house, he thought – or maybe in one of the outbuildings. There were several barns and a garage.

"Do you want to come with us, Magnus?" Jupiter asked him. Since Magnus was generally a gloomy sort of person, Jupiter didn't think he'd say yes.

"I'll stay in the truck, I think," Magnus said. "But thanks for asking."

The three capybaras were behind a wire fence, still grazing, and still close to the edge of the pond. Pete started laughing with pleasure when he saw them. Bob chuckled, and even Jupiter found the sight of the giant rodents disarming.

They were about four feet long and two feet high, like miniature ponies, with reddish brown coats, blunt black-tipped noses, narrow heads, straight, sloped foreheads, and two smallish in-turned ears. When they saw the boys opening the gate and letting themselves into the field, the capybaras stopped grazing and looked interested. One started loping toward them, and Pete was soon on his knees next to it, hugging it.

"Aren't they great?" Pete exclaimed delightedly. "They seem to really like people."

"They do," Jupiter admitted, as the other

two capybaras now also made their way over to the boys, and he and Bob each had a capybara to pet.

"I want one!" Pete said fervently, with his face buried in the capybara's back.

"From the reading we did, you'd need to get several, and you'd have to ask your father to turn your backyard into a wetlands," Jupiter said. "Besides, they're illegal in California."

"But capybaras could never become an invasive species in California," protested Pete. "It's too dry here! They couldn't survive here unless they were being taken care of by someone. I really think they should be allowed!"

"You may be right," Jupiter said. "The problem with laws and regulations is that once they're on the books, they're very hard to get off again, even if they have no utility."

"What does that mean?" Pete asked.

"No usefulness," Jupiter said.

Jupiter was watching Pete scratch his capybara on its long sloping forehead when a man suddenly emerged from a fading red barn about a hundred yards away.

The man walked toward the fenced enclosure in a hostile manner, and Jupiter told Pete and Bob that all three of them should get outside the fence again. Since there had been a public sale at the property this morning, it had never occurred to Jupiter that anyone would object to their presence, but from what he could see, someone did.

By the time they were closing the gate behind them, the man was close enough to see properly. He was in his early fifties, and looked surly – even a bit threatening.

"Holy guacamole," Pete said in a half-whisper. "I just met this guy this morning. His name is Slade something, and he's a member of some band called Existential Evil. They were practicing in our neighborhood."

As the man strode toward them, Jupiter decided to take the initiative.

"Hello," he said, walking toward the man with his hand stretched out. "You must be Mr. Tate's son?"

The man stopped short and put his hands on his hips.

"You must be incorrect," he said.

Jupiter was taken aback by the man's rudeness. "My uncle was here earlier – ."

"Yeah?" the man said. "Well, what do you want?" He reached up and began to finger the gold cross around his neck, flipping it between his fingers. He'd shaved his head, and his bald dome was disconcerting.

"Actually, my friends and I just came out to see the capybaras," Jupiter said. The man was staring at him with an animosity that made him uneasy. "Do you know where Mr. Tate got them?"

"You'd have to talk to Russell," the man said. "I don't know anything about that. Anyway, they're already taken. A guy's supposed to get here any minute to pick them up."

As if on cue, Jupiter heard the sound of tires on gravel and turned to see a white panel truck driving up the driveway, a cloud of dust trailing behind it.

"Here he is now," the man said. The panel truck with Texas plates pulled up not far from the Salvage Yard truck, and a second man got out. He was wearing blue jeans and cowboy boots and a pearl-buttoned shirt. He looked from Jupiter to the man with the chain.

"You must be Slade," he said, sticking out his hand. The man Jupiter had been talking to shook it grimly and got right down to business.

"You got cages for the giant pigs?" he said.

The man flung open the back doors of the panel truck to reveal three large cages.

The floor was strewn with hay and there were large water dishes in each cage.

"You got a ramp?" Slade asked.

The Texan took a sturdy iron ramp out of the back and attached it.

"So we'll just put a rope around them and drag them up," Slade said. "Glad to see the last of them."

By this time, Pete and Bob had gathered around and Magnus had gotten out of the Salvage Yard truck and was looking on.

"Hi," Pete said to the Texan. "Can I ask you a question?"

"Sure, son," the man said.

"Are these your first capybaras?"

The man smiled. "I've got a small herd back home near Austin," the man said. "These new ones will fit in real well."

Jupiter was glad to hear that. Whether or not Mr. Tate had known that capybaras were illegal in California, he had obviously taken good care of these three, and from the evidence, their new owner would as well.

"Do these boys work for you?" the Texan asked Slade.

Slade laughed harshly. "Never seen them before in my life," he said. "You bring the cash?" He put his hand on the man's shoulder, turned him away, and began walking with him toward the fenced field.

"Hey," Pete said angrily. "You saw me this morning." But Slade paid no attention.

Jupiter watched them go. There was no particular reason that this man Slade should have been friendly to him and Pete, but he seemed to have gone out of his way to be brusque, unpleasant, and condescending. From what Jupiter had seen so far, he had little reason to condescend.

Still, it was clear to Jupiter that if they stayed any longer he would have another confrontation with Slade, so he suggested they head back to the truck. Before they got in, they examined Walter Tate's aviary – a series of three large, connected, now-empty outdoor cages with a concrete base. Each cage was about fifteen feet long by fifteen feet wide and as many feet high. They were made of thick wire mesh, and each had a domed top. The individual cages were connected by tunnels of wire, so a bird would have been able to fly from one to the next.

Though the aviary was empty of birds, it was still filled with branches and perches and hanging swings and ladders and bells on lengths of ribbon. A few unsold bird cages were piled outside, but they, too, had no birds in them. Jupiter and his friends had just turned away from the aviary and back toward the Salvage Yard truck when the front door of the house opened and a second man appeared.

"That's the other guy!" said Pete. "The other member of Existential Evil! Slade plays bass guitar and this guy's the lead singer."

There wasn't time for Pete to say more, because the man was soon beside them.

"Hello again," he said to Pete. "Fancy meeting you here." He was wearing sunglasses, a flowered Hawaiian shirt, and a black fedora, and seemed, at first glance, a completely different kind of person from Slade. Although he, too, was strong and muscled, the only part of him that really seemed excessive − or at least unusual − was his jutting jaw.

He glanced at Magnus, now back sitting in the truck, then waved and called out to him, "Hi, how are ya?"

He turned his attention to the boys. "I'm Russell Tate," he said, in a strangely twangy accent. "I saw you looking at the aviary. The birds have all been sold, but if you're interested in coming back next Saturday, we're having a sale of items from the house."

"We just came to see the capybaras,"

Jupiter said. "My uncle was out this morning buying some bird cages and other stuff, and he told us about them."

Quite effortlessly, Jupiter had adopted his stupider-than-I-look persona. He found it useful in situations like this one.

"It's too bad we have to let them go," said Russell. "An ex-student of my father's found them by the side of the road and convinced him to take them on. I was a bit worried the police would show up and haul him off to prison, but they didn't."

He chuckled, then looked over to where Slade and the Texan were just completing the process of loading the capybaras into the Texan's truck.

"So which one was your uncle?" he said, turning back to Jupiter, and taking off his sunglasses.

He looked at Jupiter straight on, and although he might have been squinting to protect himself from the sun, when Jupiter saw him from this new angle, he thought his eyes looked hard and mean. Though he was still smiling broadly, it was a forced smile, Jupiter thought, and when he spoke, his lips were curled up at the edges. Between the flamboyant clothes, the hard eyes, and the phony smile, all of a sudden Walter Tate's son did not look to Jupiter like a man you could trust, and he decided to lie about his uncle.

"He was the tall thin guy in his early forties wearing rectangular blue-rimmed glasses and driving a white panel van. My aunt was with him. She's Cuban," Jupiter said.

Before Pete or Bob could register surprise, Jupiter added, in a very firm tone, "Anyway, thanks for the tip about next Saturday. If my uncle decides to come back for the sale, we'll come with him. It was nice to meet you. Goodbye for now."

As confidently as he could, he turned and briskly led the way to the Salvage Yard truck, then climbed into it, closely followed by Pete and Bob. He was happy to note that neither one of them said or did anything unusual that might be observed by Russell Tate, although as soon as the truck had left the Tate property, they both started asking questions at once.

"Why did you give him that bogus description of your uncle?" Pete asked.

"Why didn't you want him to know who you were?" asked Bob. "It was lucky your uncle came in the big truck with Leif, and we went back in the small one with Magnus, or he would have known who we were at once."

"I really can't explain it," Jupiter said. "Not rationally at least. But there was something about Russell Tate I didn't like. I might not even have noticed how I felt if we hadn't already had a run-in with that other guy, but Slade was such a nasty character that when I saw Russell looking over at him, my antennae went up.

"Of course, I don't know what the relationship between the two of them is, but the look Russell gave Slade made it seem like he was a boss checking to see his overseer was on the job. And the way Slade said, 'You bring the cash?' to the Texan made me think it wasn't the first time he'd used those words."

"He *was* pretty shady," Pete admitted.

"How would you get capybaras into California?" Bob asked. "I didn't see the look you saw on Russell Tate's face, but, to me, his father's property wasn't the kind of place that would have illegal activity going on. I wish we'd met *him,* not just his son," he added.

Jupiter thought for a minute. "Perhaps we can find out the name of the retirement community he's living in," he said. "There can't be that many in Rocky Beach, and if the two of you are free tomorrow morning, I'll do my best to find out which one he's moved to. If I find it, we can visit him."

"But we don't know him at all!" Pete exclaimed. "Would they even let us in to see him? And if they did, maybe he'd think it was rude of us to be prying into his personal business, or asking him about his son."

"We wouldn't have to do that," Bob said. "And he might even like the company. After all, his wife just died six months ago, and Uncle Titus told us that his daughter lives in Sacramento."

"That's true," Pete said. "Well, I'm up for it, if you are. And if you can find out where he is."

"I'm sure I can," said Jupiter.

He thought for another minute, then added to Bob, "Maybe tonight you could do more research on how capybaras might be getting to California from South America."

"O.K., boss," Bob said.

Jupiter smiled briefly, then pinched his lip and looked out the window of the truck. Was he overreacting to what first Slade and then Russell Tate had said and done? Would it be rude for him and Pete and Bob to simply drop in on Walter Tate unannounced?

But though these questions drifted briefly

through Jupiter's mind, the question he couldn't dislodge for the whole ride back to the Salvage Yard was whether or not The Three Investigators had, in fact, stumbled on a new case – and one that involved the illegal animal trade.

3

Rafael and Rojo

That night, after dinner, Bob did the research Jupiter had asked him to do, and although he discovered nothing conclusive about how the three capybaras who were now on their way to Texas might have arrived in California to begin with, he discovered more than he'd ever wanted to know about the illegal wildlife trade.

As he sat at his desk reading article after article, Bob was particularly disturbed to find that a lot of Chinese actually still believed that ground-up animal bones or teeth or extracts from certain specific organs of certain specific endangered animals could increase their longevity or fertility. China was the country from which his mother's parents had fled in the 1960s, and although Bob knew that neither he nor his family was in any way implicated in this horrible trade, he couldn't help but feel obscurely guilty.

He felt bad in a different way when he read that the Chinese also had an apparently insatiable desire for the swim bladders of a huge Mexican fish called the totoaba. It lived only in the Sea of Cortez — the thin stretch of water between the western coast of Mexico and Baja California — and it was on the brink of extinction because a lot of Chinese wanted the swim bladders — inflatable pouches that helped keep the giant fish afloat — for fish maw soup.

The swim bladders were all they wanted, it seemed; the fish were thrown away. Not only that, but Mexican fisherman used huge nets called gill nets to catch the totoaba, so a lot of other kinds of fish and a porpoise called the vaquita got caught in the nets by accident.

Because of this, vaquitas were now the most critically endangered marine mammal on the planet, Bob read. Since a single totoaba swim bladder could sell for ten thousand American dollars — a fortune for a poor Mexican fisherman — if the Chinese didn't stop making fish maw soup, both the totoaba and the vaquita would soon be gone forever.

Bob slept badly that night — so badly that the next morning at breakfast he decided to talk to his mother about what he'd read. Because his mother was an evolutionary biologist, although she could be hard to talk to about non-scientific things, when it came to stuff like this she was great.

"I don't know, Mom," said Bob, as he

ate his cereal. "The Chinese connection to all this animal smuggling really made me feel awful."

"It makes me feel that way, too," she said, shaking her head. "But human beings evolved as predators and even now have a powerful evolutionary instinct to think of other animals as prey. It isn't easy to overcome that instinct, and in China a cultural inclination toward conformity has always made it hard for people to argue with ancient wisdom."

"But it *wasn't* wisdom!" Bob said. "Not really. All those animal parts never helped people live longer or made them more fertile! And this fish maw soup is supposed to balance yin and yang energy. There's got to be some other way to do *that*!"

"I agree with you completely," his mother said. "But things are changing, even in China. The impulse to mutual aid and understanding is a strong evolutionary force, too, and photography and nature documentaries have helped a lot. They've let people see what they could never really see before – how similar other animals are to *us*. Don't worry. We're going to get there, eventually."

"I hope you're right, Mom," Bob said, a little gloomily.

Even so, by the time breakfast was over, Bob felt a lot more optimistic. Up in his bedroom, he thrust his laptop into his backpack and turned on his flip-top phone. He was surprised when the phone starting ringing just after he'd zipped it into its special pouch. He took it out again to see that someone named R. Solares was calling. R. Solares? Bob wondered. Maybe this was the guy Pete had met in the bird shop!

"Hello?" he said. "Bob Andrews speaking."

"Hello, Bob," a deep voice said. "This is Rafael Solares. When I was in Veronica's Exotic Birds the other day, I met your friend Pete Crenshaw. He gave me a Three Investigators business card, which is how I got your number. I'd like to meet with all three of you about a possible case. Would now be an O.K. time?"

Since Bob had never spoken to Rafael Solares before, he didn't know what his voice normally sounded like, but it seemed to him there was a hint of something like worry hiding in it somewhere.

"I'm not at the Salvage Yard at the moment," Bob said, "but I should be there in about fifteen minutes. Pete and Jupiter will already be there, Mr. Solares."

"Please call me Rafael," he said. "I'll see you soon."

"All right," Bob said. "Bye." He slipped the phone back in its special pocket, said good-bye to his mother, and climbed onto his bike. A case! he thought. At least maybe. And one that Pete had somehow stumbled onto in a bird shop! Fifteen minutes later, he was gliding through the wrought-iron gates that framed the entrance to the Salvage Yard.

Although he was eager to tell Pete and Jupiter the news, instinctively, he looked to see if Mallory MacLeod's bike was there before re-membering that she'd gone out of town for a few days with her mother.

Mallory had moved to Rocky Beach from Scotland at the end of her school year, and she'd become friends with the Three Inves-tigators and had helped them on three of their last four cases.

She'd also gotten a job working for Jupi-ter's Aunt Mathilda, inventorying and listing online the best of what the Salvage Yard had to offer.

Bob found Jupiter and Pete in the out-door workshop.

"There you are," said Jupiter. "We've discovered where Walter Tate moved to. He's at a place called Evergreen Retirement Community, and we should be able to get there by bike in twenty minutes."

"We might want to hold off leaving just now," Bob said. "Right before I left my house, I got a call from Rafael Solares. He wants to meet with us, and he's on his way."

"Rafael Solares?" Pete exclaimed. "I thought he might call us, but I couldn't be sure!"

"Why did you give him our card to begin with?" Jupiter asked. "Your story about him buying a scarlet macaw for a lot less than it was worth intrigued me, but I didn't follow up."

"But that's just it!" Pete exclaimed. "When Veronica said she wondered why a Mexican man who spoke no English would be selling a scarlet macaw for $300, Rafael said he wondered, too. He said he wished he could look into the matter. So my mother urged me to give him one of our cards – because we investigate anything!"

"Very true," said Jupiter.

"He told me I reminded him of his son," Pete said. "Rafael lives in Santa Barbara, but his son lives with his mother somewhere near the Mexican border."

"Is Rafael Mexican?" Jupiter asked.

"No, he's American," said Pete. "And though I guess one of his parents *was* Mexican, the other one was Chumash. Chumash Indian. That's what Veronica said, anyway. And his pickup is painted with symbols copied from Chumash paintings in a cave up the coast."

Bob's father was a journalist for the Los Angeles *Sun* and since he'd written an article about the Chumash once, Bob actually knew something about them. At the moment all that came to mind was that in one of the Chumash origin myths a goddess had built a rainbow bridge to take some of the Chumash from their home on the Channel Islands to the California mainland. If Bob was remembering correctly, when some of them fell off the bridge into the ocean, she turned them into dolphins to save them from drowning.

Bob's father had told him this explained why the Chumash called dolphins their brothers and sisters. He'd also told Bob the Chumash believed that the brightest stars in the sky were gods and the dimmer ones were the souls of the dead.

"I don't know anything about the Chumash," said Jupiter.

"That's not surprising," Bob said.

"There are only five thousand people left who claim descent from the original tribes, and their language is classified as lost. My dad did a feature article about the last native speaker of the Chumash language, who died in the 1960s."

Just then, they all heard the sound of tires on gravel and Bob turned to see an old battered pickup pull into the Salvage Yard. Its front fender was dented, it had a long crease down the length of the passenger side, and it was covered with dings, scratches, and dimples, but it was painted yellow and bore cheerful symbols.

Pete waved vigorously, then led the way to the truck where Bob saw a man starting to clamber out of the driver's seat. In the passenger seat − belted in with a seatbelt − was a cage holding a scarlet macaw. As the man climbed out, he called, "Hey, Pete." He had long jet-black hair pulled back in a ponytail held with a silver clip, and he wore a loose-fitting shirt and jeans. Bob stepped forward to shake his hand.

"We just spoke on the phone," he said.

"So you're Bob," Rafael said, "and you must be Jupiter." He shook his hand, too. "I'm glad to meet both of you."

He walked around his truck, opened the

passenger door, and unbuckled the bird cage. He came back holding the cage in one hand and a small paper bag in the other.

"Why did you bring Rojo?" Pete asked.

Rafael looked at him a little wryly. "Because I'm hoping that if he sees you again, he'll make the same racket he made the other day after I left him at Veronica's. She hasn't heard him do any of that since."

"It's pretty hot in the sun," Jupiter said. "Why don't we take Rojo to our outdoor workshop? It's right over here."

Everyone followed Jupiter to the workshop, but once they arrived, instead of settling down, Jupiter startled Bob by suggesting that all four of them go into Headquarters. Jupiter wasn't in the habit of inviting total strangers into the old mobile home trailer The Three Investigators had converted into a Headquarters. In fact, as far as Jupiter was concerned, only he, Pete, and Bob had any business ever going in there.

For some reason, today was different. They went in through Easy Three – an old oak door in its frame which was the entrance to Headquarters they used most of the time these days. Jupiter led the way. Once inside, Bob opened the trapdoor in the ceiling to let in light and air, Jupiter opened a window, and Pete turned on the oscillating fan, then went back outside and returned with one of the green metal chairs from the outdoor workshop.

It was funny, but until this moment, Bob had hardly even considered that there had been a bird like Rojo in Headquarters once before. For a while a mynah bird called Blackbeard had been a mascot of The Three Investigators, living in the old trailer until he was given to a bird-loving friend of Jupiter's Aunt Mathilda. His full name had been Blackbeard the Pirate, and he had been fond of saying "Yo ho ho and a bottle of rum." The first time Pete had ever met him, he had bitten Pete's ear. There was still a hook in the ceiling from which they'd hung Blackbeard's cage.

Almost as though he knew this, Rafael hung Rojo's cage from the hook, then opened the paper bag he was carrying. In it was a water bottle and a sack of food. As the four of them settled into chairs, Rojo suddenly opened his beak and squawked. "More capybaras on the way!" he said.

All four of them stared at the bird in surprise, but it was Rafael who had the presence of mind to speak first.

"Well, *that* was a good instinct of mine,"

he said. "I thought that hearing Pete again might do the trick. You must be good with animals," he said to him.

Pete looked a bit embarrassed but for once didn't actually blush.

"Well, I sure like them," he said. "I've started volunteering at an animal rescue center in town. And after you left the store the other day, my mother bought me a couple of lovebirds."

"Every young man should have animals to care for," Rafael said, nodding seriously.

"Is that why you said I reminded you of your son?" Pete asked. "He's an animal lover, too?"

For a moment, Rafael looked almost tense, and Bob was reminded of the worried tone in his voice during their phone conversation. But Rafael just shook his head. "It wasn't that exactly," he said. He paused for a moment, as if he were about to say something else – or something more – but then stopped himself and fell silent.

"Anyway," Pete said. "I'm glad you heard Rojo say that thing about capybaras. Yesterday I woke up never having heard of them, and now they're coming out of the woodwork! Have you ever seen one?" he asked.

"Yes," said Rafael. "Two years ago I found three capybaras not far from Isla Vista, where I live. I took them to an old friend of mine who has a house in the country. Or had."

Now it was The Three Investigators' turn to fall silent.

"Was your old friend with a house in the country named Walter Tate, by any chance?" Jupiter interjected.

Rafael looked surprised.

"You know Wally?" he said.

"We were actually about to go and try to meet him," Jupiter said. "But then Bob told us you were on your way. My uncle who owns the Salvage Yard bought a number of birdcages at a sale at his property yesterday. We went over in the afternoon to see the capybaras."

Although Bob was pretty certain he'd already guessed, he asked, "How do you know Mr. Tate?"

"I grew up in Rocky Beach," Rafael said, "and I went to Rocky Beach High."

"We're starting there next month!" Pete said.

"It's an excellent school," said Rafael. "And I was lucky to have Walter Tate as my English teacher the very last year he taught there. We really got along. He invited me to his retirement party. I loved his wife Patricia from the start and I also liked his daughter Cynthia, who lives in Sacramento now. I guess Wally's recently moved to some place called the Evergreen Retirement Community."

"If you hadn't called me when you did, we'd be knocking on his door by now," Bob said.

Bob had reacted to Russell Tate pretty much the way that Jupiter had, and later Pete had told them both about the encounter he'd had with Russell's garage band. Still, by now he was old enough to know that fathers and sons could be very different, and he was curious to meet a man who'd taught English for many years at the high school he'd be going to in the fall.

"I've been planning to visit him, too," said Rafael, "but I've been busy up until today. We're pretty tight – though very different. I'd say he's a skeptic and a rationalist, and I tend to be drawn to the mystical side of things."

"That's what made you think Rojo might talk if he saw me again," Pete said.

Before Rafael had a chance to answer, there was another squawk from overhead and Rojo erupted into his repertoire of noises – one after the other. Before he'd gotten very far, Bob was inspired to grab the Three Investigators' digital recorder, which was on the desk, and switch it on.

Rojo whooshed and creaked, he made a noise like a siren, and then he sounded like a pull-cord lawnmower straining to start. Rafael was staring at Rojo in amazement and Pete was laughing when suddenly the bird started making noises that sounded to Bob like music — a kind of trilling, a sequence of notes that rose in sequence, one after the other, then fell. Whenever Bob imagined that he was on the verge of deciphering a regular pattern, the bird stopped and started again.

Bob looked at Pete questioningly, but Pete shook his head. "No," he said. "I've never heard *that* before."

Then Rojo cawed sharply and whistled and made a noise that sounded like nothing so much as a distant squabble of seagulls. He stretched his neck as high as the cage would allow, ruffled his feathers, and settled back down, as though he had never made a sound.

"You got all that on the recorder?" Jupiter asked.

"Yes," Bob said. "He repeated himself enough so I'm sure I got it all."

"That was indeed an odd assemblage of

noises," Jupiter said. "When Pete got back from the bird shop and imitated Rojo, I was quite impressed. But hearing the sounds from the bird himself has been helpful. The creaking sound was slow and rhythmic, and the whooshing noise sounded like wind and water. What if the engine Pete interpreted as a lawnmower was really an outboard motor?"

"An outboard motor!" said Pete. "Of course! That would make total sense! Along with the whooshing and creaking!"

"Of course it doesn't explain that strange trilling, but at the very end, Rojo almost sounded like seagulls calling," Bob agreed.

"So maybe the man Rafael bought Rojo from kept him on a sailboat!" Pete exclaimed.

"Maybe," said Rafael a little doubtfully. "But he seemed to be a man who wouldn't own one. Or rather, a man who *couldn't* own one. He seemed far too poor for that. However, I can't help but agree with you that there was something distinctly nautical about the sounds the bird just made."

"Still," said Jupiter, "He *could* have lived on a boat. It's a good hypothesis – pending further investigation. In the meantime can you tell us a little more about how you came to buy him, and why you were worried about it? Pete gave us the short version but I'd like to hear the long one."

"Well," said Rafael, "I was at the farmer's market in town, and I saw a Mexican man holding a piece of cardboard with FOR SALE $300 on it. Rojo was in a cage on the ground in front of him."

"And you knew that the price was very low for such a bird?" Jupiter said

Rafael nodded. "Much too low. I started asking the man questions, but he had a weak smile on his face and kept shaking his head, so I understood that he knew little English. I switched to Spanish and he told me his name was José and introduced me to Rojo – who he said he'd inherited from an uncle."

"José?" Pete said. "I just met a Mexican guy named José yesterday. Down at the marina near the bird shop." He hastened to add, "I'm not saying it's the same José. I know a lot of men are called that in Mexico."

"You can say that again," Rafael said, smiling. "If you throw some pebbles in Mexico, you're bound to hit six Josés. Anyway, the José I was talking to said he had to sell the bird because the building he was living in wouldn't let him keep it. When I asked him where he lived, he told me he couldn't remember. It didn't take much to figure out that he was making up his story."

"You mean about his uncle?" Pete asked.

"For sure about where he lived," Rafael said. "His story was so suspicious I wondered if maybe he'd stolen the bird."

"That seems like a logical conclusion," Jupiter said.

"After that, he just kept smiling and pointing at Rojo and repeating 'Tres hondred.'"

"It seems he wasn't very quick on his feet," Jupiter said.

"So I got a little worried," Rafael said. "He was quite insistent that he wanted to part with Rojo, and I became concerned that if he couldn't unload him, he might just abandon him. Or sell him to someone who wouldn't take proper care."

Rafael paused. "Anyway, when I met Pete at Veronica's, I got the idea that maybe you guys could investigate the man I bought Rojo from. But by the time I called Bob, I'd decided he really couldn't be a smuggler. After all, anyone trafficking in scarlet macaws would have a far better system for selling illegal birds than poor José seemed to have."

Well, *that* was interesting, Bob thought. If Rafael had decided that the man who'd sold Rojo wasn't involved in the illegal animal trade, he'd come to the Salvage Yard for some other reason. He, Pete, and Jupiter all looked at him expectantly, but once again it was Jupiter who surprised him.

"Whatever brought you here today, I'm glad you came," he said. "But I'm also a little puzzled. Why would you trust perfect strangers with an investigation that mattered to you — particularly strangers who haven't even turned fourteen?"

Rafael smiled. "A hunch," he said. "I have good instincts when it comes to people. I work as a special education teacher for the Santa Barbara school system. I'm drawn to animals in need. Human animals, too."

"Wow!" Pete said. "Veronica at the bird shop told my mother and me that you were some sort of envoy for the Chumash in the Santa Barbara schools, but she didn't say you were a teacher! My mom teaches fifth grade."

"Fifth-graders are great," Rafael said, "but I have students from lots of different grades. The Chumash envoy thing is just a part-time gig — one I sometimes wonder whether I should have accepted. After all, I'm just as much Spanish as I am Chumash."

"I know what you mean," said Bob. "I'm just as Scottish as I am Chinese – but a lot of times other people can't see that."

Rafael. laughed. "Since the last native Chumash speaker died in the 1960's, I guess in *my* case they'll take what they can get."

"Bob was telling us earlier about an article his father wrote for the Los Angeles *Sun*," Jupiter said. "It's terrible that the Chumash language is now classified as lost."

"Well, yes, and no," said Rafael. "In one way, of course it is – not least because when we lost the language we lost a lot of the history of the people who spoke it. On the other hand, words get lost and are changed all the time, and anything that makes communication between different sorts of people possible would seem to be a good thing."

"That's true, I suppose," said Jupiter. He paused. "So what *did* bring you here today?"

"A much more personal mystery than the mystery of Rojo and his noises," said Rafael. "I wasn't sure I'd tell you this, but the three of you have impressed me since I got here. I wish my son had friends like you down in Chula Vista. And since you and he are about the same age – well, I somehow feel I can trust you to find out the truth. I'm afraid Gabriel is involved with a man who works in Veronica's bird shop – helping to smuggle exotic birds into California."

As Rafael said this, Bob happened to be looking at Pete – and Pete looked even more stunned than Bob felt.

4

A Troubled Son

And Pete *was* stunned. He'd been expecting Rafael to say something pretty personal after telling them he was impressed with The Three Investigators, but this was a total shock. For once, Pete was speechless.

Luckily, Jupiter wasn't.

"Let's start with the man who works in Veronica's bird shop," Jupiter said. "Who is he, and why do you suspect him?"

Pete remembered him, working in the back of the shop. Curly blond hair and a soul patch.

"His name is Jack Cutter," Rafael said. "And this morning, when I was talking to Veronica about Rojo, he interrupted our conversation to say that he thought that capybaras should be legal in California."

"Just like that?" Jupiter asked.

"Just like that," Rafael said. "I agreed with him, of course. Almost anyone sensible would. Walter Tate certainly did when I took him the capybaras I found up near Santa Barbara. He said he was old enough not to worry about minor legal infractions any longer. Still, it wasn't so much the remark Cutter made as the fact that he approached me and Veronica when we were clearly having a private conversation.

"He's been working at Veronica's for a while now, and the last time I went through Rocky Beach, about six months ago, Gabriel was with me – I was bringing him back to his mother after a two-week visit with me up in Isla Vista – and he and Jack Cutter seemed to really hit it off.

"The truth is, ever since Gabriel's mother and I broke up and she moved down to Chula Vista, my relationship with Gabriel has been getting worse and worse," Rafael said. "It hasn't been good for him not to have a father around. And even though I've tried to teach him that people should be kind to animals since he was really young – and not just because animals can suffer as much as people can, but also because cruelty is bad for the soul! – about a year ago, I found out he'd gotten involved in cockfighting."

"Cockfighting!" Pete exclaimed, aghast.

"Yes," said Rafael grimly. "Still, I never would have imagined he'd get caught up in animal smuggling. But when he met Cutter, that was what they ended up talking about. I was with Veronica, and the two of them were off in a corner laughing about something. I don't know what, but later on, I know they were talking about the illegal trade in hyacinth macaws. You remember Agatha?" he asked Pete.

Pete nodded.

"Well, from what I overheard of the conversation, my son seemed to think it was too bad that wild macaws like Agatha weren't still being imported from the Pantanal − and when he said that, Cutter gave off this very weird vibe. I thought maybe you could find out more about him − follow him home or research his background on the Internet," said Rafael.

"What does this Cutter look like?" Jupiter asked.

"He's in his late twenties," Rafael said. "Blond hair in a short ponytail. He's got a little tuft of beard under his lower lip. His ears stick out a bit."

Pete was sure he'd recognize him, but he really didn't think he'd remember seeing Pete.

"Do you have any reason to think he's dangerous?" Jupiter asked Rafael.

"Not really," Rafael said. "He has no menace to him."

"As for your son, has he said or done anything other than talk to Jack Cutter about hyacinth macaws that has made you suspicious?" Jupiter asked.

"Yes and no," Rafael said. "When I met Pete at Veronica's, I'd just taken Gabriel back to Chula Vista, and while we were there I went to his room – where I found about fifteen hyacinth macaw feathers. I couldn't stop myself from asking where he'd gotten them, and why he was keeping them in his room, and he said that a friend of his mother's had given them to him. But when I asked her if that was true, she claimed she'd never seen them before."

The more Rafael talked about the situation with his son, the sorrier Pete felt for him. When he'd first met him, at the bird shop, he'd felt at once that Rafael was not simply a trustworthy guy, but a good one, and it seemed really unfair that he and his son couldn't live together. Although Pete's father was away from home a lot, working on movies, he came home at least every two weeks, and he and Pete had always been close.

Not as close as Pete and his mother, but still, really tight. It was awful to think that a kid who might be a lot like him almost never saw his father. Seeing your father was important.

"I see," said Jupiter. "So the only plausible way to get a sense of whether your son and Jack Cutter are actually connected – and doing something illegal together – would be to approach it from the Cutter end. We'd be happy to do what we can. And maybe Walter Tate could shed more light on the situation with the capybaras."

"If you want, I can drive you over to where he's living now and introduce you," Rafael said.

Pete and Bob deferred to Jupiter at moments like this, so Pete was glad that Jupiter agreed without a moment's hesitation.

"What about Rojo?" Pete asked.

"Maybe you guys could look after him for a day or two," Rafael said. "He'd be quite all right in your Headquarters as long as you leave the windows open, and visit him from time to time. Make sure he has plenty of food and water. Who knows? Maybe he'll add something new to his repertoire!"

Pete followed the others out through Easy Three and back into the Salvage Yard. There, he had a sudden thought. "Wait," he said. "Before we go, there's something you might want to see. It's a box of stuff Jupiter's Uncle Titus bought at the sale at Mr. Tate's place. Wood carvings and ceramic birds."

"I'm sure you can call him Wally," Rafael said.

Jupiter led the way. The box was just inside one of the sheds, and when Rafael saw its contents, he shook his head in dismay.

"Who sold these to your uncle?" he asked. "Some of these were made by Patricia and some by Wally's daughter Cynthia, and I'd be surprised if he really wanted to sell them."

"Uncle Titus told us he bought them from the owner's son," Jupiter said. "We met him yesterday afternoon when we went out. He was there with a man named Slade. Do you know him?"

"I don't," said Rafael. "But I do know Russell, and I've never liked him. His mother and sister were both real artists, but he's always struck me as a phony. Everyone needs money, but even so, I'm amazed he would sell his mother's and sister's work."

He picked up the carving of the humpback whale that Pete had noticed yesterday and had liked so much.

"This, on the other hand, was carved by a Chumash friend of mine," Rafael said. "I gave it to Patricia as a present and she loved it.

I'd like to buy it back, if I could."

Pete looked forward to seeing Jupiter bargain. He'd watched it before and it was very entertaining. But this time, to Pete's surprise, Jupiter said, "You can have it. I'm sure my uncle and aunt won't mind."

Pete wasn't so sure about Aunt Mathilda. She'd been quite firm about Lief putting the carving down. But he didn't say anything.

"Thanks a lot. That's great," Rafael said. "Well, let's go."

Rafael's truck had only a single bench seat in the front, and Jupiter suggested that Bob sit in the cab, while he and Pete climbed into the back. Pete thought it was great back there. The roof of the truck cap was high and pointed, there were colorful rugs on the floor, curtains pulled to either side of the windows, and lots of pillows and cushions. The side windows of the truck cap were open, letting in light and air.

Although it would have taken them twenty minutes to get to the Evergreen Retirement Community on their bikes, it was only about ten minutes by truck. The place was smaller than Pete had expected, and a lot more welcoming than some of the places he'd seen. The main apartment building was flanked by

flower beds filled with purple petunias, red sal-
via, and orange marigolds, and some of the
apartments had window boxes or bird feeders
outside them.

Wrapped around the building was a garden with walking paths and benches, and, inside, the lobby was filled with bright colors and
comfortable chairs. The young woman at the
reception desk was Hispanic, pretty and cheerful. Rafael asked for Walter Tate and was
given his apartment number – 207 – and direc-
tions to get there. In no time, Rafael was
knocking on his door.

Almost immediately, a strong male voice
called out, "Come in!"

Rafael pushed the door open and the
four of them stepped inside. Though Pete could
see that the apartment was institutional in its
basic outlines, it still had a comfortable, homey
feeling. One wall had a bookcase crammed
with books, while the other walls were crowded
with colorful prints and paintings. The sofa was
covered with a butter-colored fabric, and the
love seat had a printed slipcover with a blue
and yellow pattern. On a corner table was a
large collection of compact discs and a port-
able music player.

In the middle of the room stood an old

man wearing loose-fitting khaki pants and a light blue chambray shirt. He was holding a four-footed cane. He peered at them through his glasses.

"Rafael Solares!" he exclaimed in a voice with an interesting twang – both like and unlike his son's, Pete thought. "Or 'Aliksaniaset.' What does that mean, again? Something typically mystical, about disappearing and reappearing far away."

"Only you would remember that, Wally," Rafael said. "In the Spanish archives, it says the word means something which is final and commences again – like the mist or fog that comes and goes."

He walked across the room and gave Walter Tate a quick hug.

"Nice to see you too, buddy," said Mr. Tate, with a combination of teasing and affection.

Walter Tate was relatively short, with a round owlish face and keen gray eyes. He was mostly bald, with a thin tonsure of hair, and the top of his head was covered with brownish spots from the sun.

"Are we interrupting something?" Rafael asked.

A quick smile flitted across Mr. Tate's

face. "I'm not spectacularly busy at the moment."

He drew out the last word in the strangest fashion and Pete blurted out, "I've never heard an accent like yours before."

Instead of being offended, Walter Tate grinned.

"My family came to California from Oklahoma at the start of the Depression, and one of my teachers used to tell me I'd never amount to anything if I couldn't lose my Okie accent. I've never been able to decide if she was right or wrong." He turned to Rafael. "Who *are* these three young men?"

"This is Jupiter Jones, and that's Pete Crenshaw and Bob Andrews," Rafael said, pulling out the card Pete had given him in the bird shop and handing it to Mr. Tate. He studied it, then set it down.

"How curious," he said. "I was just thinking that — with the exception of the excellent staff in this establishment — the young generation these days lacks almost all get-up-and-go. Well, isn't this something? Come sit down and tell me why you're here."

He gestured to the sofa and love seat, and then — with an agility that surprised Pete quite a lot — he settled himself in a   brown leather reclining chair while the rest of them found places on the other furniture. Once seated, Pete listened as Jupiter explained about the sale at Mr. Tate's property, his uncle's purchases, and their visit to see the capybaras.

The whole time, Jupiter kept referring to their host as "Mr. Tate" until he interrupted.

"Don't make me feel more ancient than I am," he said. "You must all call me Wally. So you were coming to visit me anyway, today, and then Rafael showed up and said he would drive you here?"

The boys all nodded.

"A happy accident," Wally said. "I met Rafael my last year of teaching at Rocky Beach High, about a million years ago. We're very different. I tend to take a dim view of human affairs and put a great emphasis on rational analysis, while Rafael − . Well, let's just say he has a lot of hope."

Pete thought he said the last word as if it were forbidden in polite company.

"But when he was my student, he asked to see my poetry, and he had the audacity to like it, thereby forever winning my heart. It was bad, of course, but I forgave his lapse of taste," Wally said.

Pete could tell that Wally was a talker

and glad to have company. He was probably a shy and private man who hid that as best he could. He was very quick-witted, and though he tried to seem grumpy, he wasn't, really, Pete thought.

"He also loved my wife Patricia, and she returned the favor, so I gave him a chance," Wally said. "For many years, Rafael was the only person I deigned to tell about my experiences in the Second World War."

Rafael – who had been sitting listening – nodded.

"We both used to smoke," Rafael said. "We'd sit and smoke on the deck overlooking the pond while Wally told me stories. About recovering from a shrapnel wound in Paris, meeting jazz musicians in Czechoslovakia, and getting into a huge Army-truck traffic jam with a hotheaded driver."

"That deck was a great confessional," Wally said. "But the view was improved when the capybaras arrived."

"Rafael told us he gave you the capybaras two years ago?" Jupiter asked.

"Yes," said Wally. "Miscreant that he is. Luckily, they were all males, so their number remained at three. They were a lot of fun, for illegal animals. My house was like a petting zoo for a while. Anyone who came by seemed to wind up in the field, kissing their silly noses."

He shook his head with grudging approval of the memory. "They were even more fun than the birds — though I had a lot more of those. I was lucky to find a Texan who was willing to keep the gift in motion by taking the capybaras."

"The gift?" Pete asked.

"Yes," Wally said. He smiled indulgently. "It's part of Rafael's spiritual practice. Or so he tells me. He gave them to me with the admonition that they must never be sold."

This surprised Pete a lot. "But they actually *were* sol – ," he began.

Although Wally was looking at him with interest, waiting for him to finish his sentence, Pete suddenly didn't want to. In fact, he was happy when Jupiter took the story over.

"When we were out at your house," Jupiter said hesitantly, "we met an unsavory character named Slade, and he took cash from the Texan, for the capybaras."

Wally stared at Jupiter in something close to disbelief. "I frankly can't believe my son turned this transaction over to Francis Slade DeMarco. Slade to his friends, who I fear are very few, but one of whom, unfortunately, is Russell. My son is not, let me say, an astute judge of character."

"This Slade guy looked like he worked out," Pete said. "He was trying to be tough."

"Francis was a wrestler in high school," Wally said. "Quite good from what I heard, with dreams of going professional. But he had no discipline; always after the quick chance; always getting drunk and smashing his car into things. I'm told he's a pretty good mechanic. He has a business he runs out of his house. Unfortunately, I've had to keep up with his history. Whenever Russell came to stay, somehow Francis would show up, too. Always right at mealtime."

"Wow," Pete said. "He sounds like bad news."

"My boy," Wally said. "There's no such thing as good news."

"I'm also sorry to tell you that Russell seems to have sold some of the carvings and pottery that Patricia and Cynthia did," Rafael said.

For a moment Wally was silent. Then he shook his head and said – more to himself than to anyone else – "I've never really trusted Russell, but Patricia loved him more than life itself."

He suddenly turned to Jupiter. "Did you see the chickens when you were at my house?" he asked.

"All the aviaries were empty," Jupiter said, "and all the cages, too."

"But you didn't check the barn?" Wally asked. "I'm suddenly worried about the chickens. I kept them in the barn. What if Russell forgot the chickens? What if they have no food or water?"

Pete could see he was really troubled by this. Obviously Wally had taken care of his animals when he'd had them.

"If it's not too much trouble," Wally said to Rafael, "maybe you could drive me out to the old estate so that I can check for myself. Alas, my driver's license has been taken by the Gestapo. Would you boys like to come along?"

That sounded great to Pete. He'd miss the capybaras, but he'd really liked Wally Tate's place − and he wanted to see some more of Rafael Solares. However, just then, Wally seemed to remember his manners and said that perhaps they should all have some food first.

"You can all be my guests in the commissary," he said.

"What's a commissary?" Pete asked.

Wally turned to him swiftly. "A grand affair, my boy, worthy of a pasha. Usually a buffet."

Everyone got to their feet, and as they walked toward the dining room or cafe or whatever it might turn out to be, Wally and his one-time student walked off to the side to conduct at least a semi-private conversation.

Even so, Pete heard every word of it, and he wasn't surprised when the two men started talking about their sons. Wally commented that Rafael had been right about Russell all along – that even though he'd hoped for a son who shared his values and his taste, it had turned out that the child he had most in common with was his daughter. When he asked Rafael how Gabriel was, Rafael told Wally the same thing he'd told The Three Investigators.

"You really think he's involved in animal smuggling?" Wally asked incredulously

"Well, of course, I don't really know," Rafael said. "But I'm worried. And even if he isn't, he's been getting more and more secretive about something. Everything, really."

"He's a teenager," Wally said. "Or maybe his mother has a new boyfriend, and doesn't want you to know, so *he* doesn't want you to know. Just hang in there, buddy. I always thought Gabriel was a good kid."

"I did, too," Rafael said. "But even if he *is* good, I wouldn't be doing him any favors if I ignored the kinds of things he's been getting into lately. Stealing hubcaps and vaping and that sort of thing."

The two men stopped talking, and as the five of them reached the commissary – which turned out to be the dining room – Pete thought back to one of the things Rafael had said earlier.

He'd said he was drawn to animals in need. "Human animals, too," was the phrase he'd used. And though of course Pete had long been aware that human beings *were* animals, he'd never before heard an adult say the phrase in a way that was respectful of human beings.

Of course, one big difference between people and other animals was that people could make choices in a way that animals really couldn't. They could make choices to help more than to harm. They could decide who to be friends with, and what they wanted to do when they grew up. They could also decide who to admire and who to distrust or dislike.

Which was why something *else* would stick in Pete's mind from the events of the day. Wally Tate had said it was part of what he'd called Rafael's "spiritual practice" to never sell an animal, or let one be sold. And although Pete could see the practical problems that might arise, he still found it a very appealing idea.

He'd been raised as a Catholic, so his early understanding of "spiritual practice" had been formed by the pomp and ceremony of the church. In fact, when he'd been eight or nine, he'd been an altar boy, dressed in red pants and a white tunic, carrying candles and the incense censor and attending Father Buchanan during the Eucharist. But the priest had been a grumbly demanding old man and Pete had grown disenchanted and stopped going to church.

At first, he'd thought he'd go back eventually – he'd felt he was taking a sort of break – and since his parents had never tried to force him to do anything he didn't feel he *should* do, they'd been fine with that.

However, since Pete still had the strong sense that there was something out there that might be called a creator – a force in the universe which had conjured parrots and capybaras and all the other amazing animals that inhabited the planet, including the human ones – during the last couple of years, Pete had realized he yearned for some sort of spiritual practice that wasn't a formal religion. Which was funny, actually, because he loved formal sports like soccer and baseball. But then, those were team sports, while thinking about creation and existence was a solitary thing.

In the dining room, Pete was soon tucking into a plateful of what Wally referred to as "passable nourishment," and Rafael called "good eats." To have met two such interesting – and different – men in a single day was a pretty unusual experience, Pete thought. After all, in their very different ways, each might be considered an excellent role model. Which was another thing human beings could do that animals probably couldn't. They could serve as exemplars that other people could emulate. He hoped that's what he himself had been the other day with Mikey.

5

Avian Banter

About forty-five minutes later, Jupiter was lying in the back of Rafael's pickup looking up at the home-made truck cap. He'd put a big pillow beneath his head, and although he didn't find the bed of a pickup truck to be his natural environment, he wasn't at all uncomfortable. Wally Tate was riding in the cab with Rafael, so this time both Pete and Bob were in the back with him. Since it was about a twenty-five minute drive to Wally's place in the country, on the way he'd have plenty of time to think.

Jupiter made a mental note to tell his uncle how pleasant the Evergreen Retirement Community was; it was far better than a term like "old age home" implied. He'd liked having lunch in the cafeteria, and the food was much heartier than he'd expected. Jupiter wondered if Wally Tate's use of the word "commissary" had been consciously ironic or an unconscious allusion to his experience in the Second World War.

Although Jupiter was no more unhappy than he was uncomfortable, he couldn't quite figure out what he was doing in Rafael Solares's truck to begin with. Usually he was in charge of events, but today events had swept him along, and he hadn't objected. This must be what people meant when they said "go with the flow," he thought. It was an unfamiliar feeling for Jupiter, but not unpleasant.

Still, one thing was for sure: His day was not unfolding as he'd expected. First a strange man whose Native American name was 'Aliksaniaset' had shown up, and then suddenly – without even thinking first – Jupiter had found himself inviting this man into Headquarters, something he would normally move heaven and earth to avoid. Once they were inside, the man had hung a talkative scarlet macaw on the hook in the ceiling as if he knew that hook had been installed to hold a birdcage — Blackbeard's, in fact.

Soon afterwards, Jupiter was listening with interest to this man lay out a possible case for The Three Investigators and somehow this had inexorably led to him offering the man a carving of a humpback whale that his uncle had just bought and that his aunt had particularly liked and admired.

Of course, if his uncle or aunt objected, he'd pay for the carving, but that wasn't the

94

point. The point was that he'd acted out of character. There was something about this guy Rafael Solares that had had a strange effect on him; instinctively he'd found himself relaxing his usual defenses.

This was sufficient cause for inquiry, and he set about asking himself questions.

Was there anything suspicious about this Rafael Solares? Jupiter thought back on everything that Rafael had said or done since he'd arrived earlier that morning − both at the Salvage Yard and at Wally Tate's. Jupiter had to admit, there was nothing faintly suspect about him. Jupiter prided himself on his ability to detect insincerity or phoniness, and so far Solares had seemed entirely genuine.

The truth was that Jupiter was enjoying the unexpected day. Riding in the back of the truck was restful, and although he knew he should probably be thinking about what he had learned about Russell Tate from first Pete, then Wally, instead his mind wandered until it finally landed on Rojo − who even now was hanging from a hook in Headquarters.

That was indeed an odd assemblage of noises the bird made, and Jupiter was pleased he had come up with a tentative explanation for them. In his mind, he sorted them out. He put "More capybaras on the way!" out of the picture for the time being, because that was simply something that Rojo had heard someone say, and it gave no clue to where it had been said. But the sounds themselves had certainly been "nautical," as Rafael had labeled them − all except for the ones that were a bit like musical notes. What on earth had *they* been, he wondered?

The truck slowed and turned, and Jupiter could see out the window that they'd arrived at Walter Tate's. They bumped down the long driveway and then they were there.

As they all got out, Jupiter found, to his surprise, that he missed the capybaras. He felt as though something vital was absent from the otherwise tidy and well-kept property.

"Well," Wally said. "It's still here. I'd like to say it's good to be back, but without Patricia, the place lacks a certain *je nais se quois*."

Jupiter felt Wally knew exactly what it was lacking but didn't want to put the feeling into words.

Although Jupiter had expected that Wally would head directly for the barn to check on the chickens, instead, with his cane in hand, he took off for the house.

"Let's get something to drink," he said as he led the way to the steps up to the L-shaped deck fronting the house and running along its side. The house itself was a Victorian, and although it might have seemed incongruous out in the country, it didn't. Its white exterior, in need of paint, was still in very good shape. Perhaps because the house had been shut up, it was pleasantly cool inside.

A long hallway ran straight from the front door to the kitchen. To the left was a living room with a fireplace and a bay window, and to the right was a room Wally said had been his wife's sewing room. At the end of the hall, just before the kitchen, there was another door Wally peered into. "And this was my study," he said.

To the right was a steep set of stairs that Jupiter assumed led to the second floor bedrooms. The carpet had seen better days and the house was a bit disarranged; Jupiter surmised that the furniture and other goods in Wally's apartment at Evergreen had been taken from these rooms. But the house had an aura of peace about it, and it didn't really seem deserted. It still seemed ready to be lived in. Or it would have if it hadn't been for the fact that almost every piece of furniture had a manilla tag with a price on it hanging from a wire.

As the others went to the kitchen, Jupiter lingered in the hallway, which was lined with photographs. In the vast majority of them, Wally Tate at various ages had shared the picture frame with his wife and two children. Patricia Tate had been a lovely woman, with intense blue eyes, a brilliant smile, and a nimbus of short curly hair. In his youth, Wally had been handsome – though not as handsome as his wife had been pretty.

Still, they seemed well suited; Mrs. Tate looked like an artist, her husband like a scholar. However, in picture after picture, although their daughter Cynthia seemed to match her parents in a kind of creative, intelligent intensity, their son Russell looked uncomfortable, or even angry, and in a good many of the pictures he had the same forced smile Jupiter had seen the day before. Though it was meant to look as if Russell was pleased to have his picture taken, that smile did not signal pleasure. He'd been bad news for a long time now, Jupiter thought.

In the kitchen, Wally had gotten five drinking glasses out of an old, hanging wall cabinet with glass doors, filled them with ice from the freezer, then held them under the tap.

"Well water," he announced. He took

one of the glasses and sipped. "Delicious," he said. Then he made his way over to an electronic thermostat and tapped it.

"You may not believe this," he said to Rafael, "but even before Patricia died, I used to spend an hour or two every day trying to figure out how to get this thing to work. It's nice and cool in the house right now, but when Patricia and I were here, it would be hot, then cold, then hot again. After Patricia died six months ago, it was almost always boiling."

He paused and thought a moment. "At least, it was boiling on hot days. On cool days, the air conditioning came on," he said. "I had the repairman in, but he was never able to establish a proper rapport with the problem. Since Russell and Cynthia thought it would be too expensive to overhaul the system, I moved out mainly to get away from this damn gadget."

"It almost sounds as if it was haunted!" Pete said. "Couldn't you have replaced it?"

"I did," Wally said. "Twice. Both times, the same thing happened, so if the thing was haunted, it was by a ghost who had no trouble moving from one gadget to a different one. Cynthia is a bit like my friend Rafael here, and she thought my thermostatic troubles were a sign from the Great Spirit that it was time for me to move somewhere else."

"What about Russell?" asked Rafael.

"*He'd* been thinking it was time for me to move somewhere else for a long time," Wally said. "Preferably the Great Beyond. I thought it was because he wanted this house, but he doesn't seem to want that at all. In fact, he seems to have big plans to go into some kind of business with a Mexican partner."

"What kind of business?" Jupiter asked.

"I didn't ask," Wally said. "His business ventures generally don't bear scrutiny." He finished his water and set the glass in the sink. "I suppose we should go to the barn now and see if the chickens have also moved on to somewhere else."

However, instead of returning to the front door by way of the center hall, Wally headed into the sitting room/dining room which lay behind the living room. There, he was arrested by the sight of the manilla price tags hanging on the furniture.

"What's this?" he said. "I thought the sale was over."

"When we met him yesterday, Russell told us the household goods were going to be sold next weekend," Bob said.

"Yes," Pete said. "And Jupiter told him we might be coming."

"Didn't you give him permission to sell these things?" Rafael asked.

Wally seemed to Jupiter either to be thinking hard or to be pretending he was doing that, since he wrinkled his forehead in puzzlement. While he was thinking, he walked around the room with his four-legged cane, lifting up price tags and dropping them.

At last he said to Rafael, "Perhaps I did. Perhaps I told him to sell whatever he wanted. I was giving things away there, for a while. I honestly don't remember. No, no, I think I do. I think I *did* tell him to sell whatever he could."

On the whole, Jupiter thought that Wally's puzzlement had been a pretense. While he clearly had long ago taken his son's meas-ure and found it wanting, he presumably didn't want to let three boys he had just met know how he felt about the matter.

The five of them walked outside, and af-ter Wally had locked the door behind them, he took off for the faded red barn with his cane in his hand. Once there, he opened the walk-in door, and Jupiter followed him. A stream of bright light pierced the shadowy interior, and as the others made their way into the barn, closing the door behind them, Jupiter could see light filtering in from high windows and cracks between the boards. Hay was piled to one side, and dust and chaff swirled in the air, its motes illuminated by streaks of light. A series of raucous squawks pierced the stillness.

As Jupiter stood there, letting his eyes adjust, he looked up at the loft, stacked with hay bales, and at the thick rafter that ran from one side of the barn to the other. He caught a hint of blue – as if there were a hole in the roof and the sky was punching through. But then his eyes adjusted more, and he watched as the patch of sky launched itself into the air. At first he couldn't quite make sense of what he was seeing. The patch had become enormous, as wide as his arms could spread, and he finally comprehended that up above him was a pair of cobalt blue wings, shining in the dimness.

"My, my," Wally said. "Look at that."

But Jupiter said nothing, and neither did anyone else. They stared in wonder as the bird soared through the heights of the barn, barely moving its wings, before pivoting and swooping down. Gracefully, it glided toward Rafael, who stuck out his arm.

The bird backpedalled with its wings and then made a perfect landing. Its clawed feet clamped around Rafael's wrist. Jupiter had never seen a bird like this one before. It was like Rojo, but a lot larger, and the intensity of its single cobalt color was astonishing.

Another squawk sounded above them. Jupiter looked up in time to see a second patch of sky spread its wings. After a slow glissade down, it landed on Rafael's left shoulder, so big its feathers brushed Rafael's ear.

"Wally," Rafael said. "I take it these birds are not yours."

"If I were the owner of two hyacinth macaws," Wally said, "do you think I'd have kept it a secret? No, those birds are not mine – though I certainly wish they were. That's about $40,000 worth of parrots you're wearing."

"I'm aware of that," Rafael said.

"Lucky as I've been in life, I was never lucky enough to be able to pay $20,000 for a single bird. And look! There are two more, in cages at the back."

Jupiter followed Wally's pointing finger and saw that, in the far back, in two cages, were two big blue birds that seemed to glow in the dimness. Two empty cages stood beside them.

"At least there are no chickens," said Rafael.

"Apparently not," Wally said. "Thank goodness for small favors. But we're going to have to take these beauties with us."

"I'm afraid so," Rafael said. "Leaving them here would not be in their best interests. I'm sure we all understand these macaws did not fly up here from Brazil on their own."

With a little coaxing, Rafael got the two loose birds back into their cages, and Jupiter, Pete, Bob, and Rafael each grabbed a cage and carried it to Rafael's truck. They loaded the birds in the back, together with a sack of food and a duffel bag of feeding bowls, water bottles, and toys.

"Where will we take them? Pete asked. "There's not enough room at Headquarters."

"No," Jupiter said, "and we shouldn't separate them. Could Veronica take them?" he asked Rafael.

"Well, she does have an aviary at home," Rafael said. "But if I'm right about Jack Cutter, then the last thing on earth we want is to let Veronica know we have them. Although she might not mean to let anyone else in on this discovery, the fewer people who know about it the better."

Jupiter thought quickly. Wally certainly couldn't bring them back to the Evergreen Retirement Community. Perhaps he could call Isabella Chang, he thought, and ask if she would take the birds temporarily.

Since the back of Rafael's truck was now crowded with hyacinth macaws, they decided that Jupiter should ride in the cab with Wally and Rafael. But before he got in, he asked Bob if he could borrow his cellphone. Bob got it out of his backpack and handed it to Jupiter.

They had just left Wally's driveway and turned onto the country road when Jupiter punched in Isabella Chang's number. The last time he'd seen her, he and Pete had gotten important information from her, in the midst of their last case, at a time when Bob hadn't been with them.

Luckily, she was home and said yes right away. She seemed truly pleased and excited, and just as Jupiter clicked the cellphone shut, it occurred to him that Wally and Isabella had a lot in common. After all, although Isabella had taught history in Palisade Point and Wally had taught English in Rocky Beach, they were both retired high school teachers. They were also both extremely smart – although Isabella's intelligence was sunnier than Wally's.

At a guess, Wally was ten years older than Isabella, but they had shared a good part of the twentieth century – including the tumultuous 1950s and 1960s – when they had both been young. As they got close to her house, Jupiter wondered if they would like each other. He didn't have to wonder long.

When Jupiter knocked, Isabella answered the door herself. Her part-time help, Charlotte Mitchell, was off today, and Isabella graciously invited all five of them in. As always, she told Jupiter, Pete, and Bob how good it was to see them. Jupiter introduced her to Wally and Rafael, and as she shook both men's hands, she looked searchingly into their faces. Neither of them knew that Isabella's sight was fading, but both of them gazed right back and held her hand until she dropped theirs.

"Come in, come in," she said as she ushered everyone into the living room. "Where are the macaws?"

"They're in the truck," Jupiter said. "We'll bring them in shortly, with your permission. But we didn't want to just arrive carrying them."

"I wouldn't have minded at all," she said.

"Jupiter tells me you taught history in Palisade Point," Wally said to Isabella.

"I taught English here in Rocky Beach, oh, about a thousand years ago. A messy business, history, isn't it? Particularly the last hundred years."

"Oh, I don't know," Isabella said. "The Middle Ages were no picnic."

"True enough," Wally said. "When one thinks about it, there's never been a good time to be alive."

Isabella laughed heartily. "I see you take a dim view of human nature."

"Perhaps if they turn the lights up, I can see it better," Wally said.

"And you taught English," Isabella said. "Are you a strict grammarian?"

"Attila the comma Hun," Wally said.

"He's really a poet," Pete said.

"Really?" Isabella said.

"Everyone's a poet," Wally said.

"I don't think so," Isabella said.

"I don't think so either," Wally said. For a while they smiled happily at one another.

"I'd like to read some of your poetry," Isabella said.

Wally looked shocked. "Over my dead body. Which I might be able to hand you any day now."

Again, Isabella laughed heartily, as

though Wally was a humorist of the rarest sort. "I would say there's considerable life in those old bones yet," she said.

Wally peered at her. "Are you flirting with me?" he asked.

Jupiter saw that this might go on for some time, so he interrupted to suggest that he, Pete, Bob, and Rafael go to the truck to get the macaws and leave Isabella and Wally together.

Isabella had covered her dining room table with a thick sheet of plastic and instructed them to put the cages right there, on top of the table.

"Oh!" she said, quite fervently. "They are beauties, aren't they?"

As if in response, one of the macaws squawked.

"They can be quite noisy, I'm afraid," Jupiter said.

"They won't bother me a bit," Isabella said. "I'm happy for the company."

Rafael explained about feeding them and keeping their water bottles full, and Isabella nodded pleasantly. She was looking at the macaws. She pointed at the one closest to her. "We could call that one Daedalion," she said.

Wally had been looking at the macaws as well, but his head snapped to the left and he was suddenly looking at Isabella with interest.

"You could call another one Philomena," he said.

Isabella smiled brilliantly at Wally. "Perhaps," she said. "But there are many other choices. Maybe Procne."

"Or Alcyone," Wally said, "from which we take the lovely word halcyon." Both of them laughed merrily.

Where were they pulling these names from? Jupiter wondered. It was as though they were speaking a secret language. For the first time in a long time, Jupiter understood the way Pete sometimes felt. Pete was standing open-mouthed. But though Jupiter kept his mouth shut, he was similarly astonished.

"But perhaps those names are too fancy," Wally said. "Perhaps we should just go with the names of our favorite Norse ravens, Huginn and Muninn!"

When Isabella saw the looks on the boys' faces, she took pity. "Mr. Tate and I were just playing one-upmanship with Greek mythology," she said.

"Call me Wally, please!" he said to Isabella. "You boys should read more Ovid! Being transformed into a bird used to be a very big thing!"

Jupiter found this charming, and was quite impressed. Clearly, Wally and Isabella had more in common than he had even thought.

They all thanked Isabella profusely and said they'd check in with her soon.

"A lovely woman," Wally said as he got in the front seat with Rafael. "I hope I see her again."

They dropped Wally off at the Evergreen Retirement Community and he thanked them all for a most interesting afternoon. Back at the Salvage Yard, they said goodbye to Rafael. Jupiter could hardly believe they'd only met the man that morning. Rafael reminded Bob that he had Rafael's number on his cellphone, and that he should call if they found out anything about Jack Cutter. He said he was staying with a sister who lived in Rocky Beach for a few days, and that he was sure he'd see them again soon.

Back in Headquarters, they checked on Rojo and refilled his water bottle. But he was fine, and he greeted the boys with his earsplitting siren noise before settling down to some gentle creaking.

Bob turned to Pete. "I'm glad we'll still have Rojo here tomorrow," he said.

"So am I," Pete said. "But why?"

"Mallory's getting back then," Bob said. "And I want her to meet him."

By now, it was late in the day and after making sure everything was shipshape in and about Rojo's cage, the three of them headed for their separate homes.

That night, before he went to sleep, Jupiter lay in bed and thought about the case. Because, by now, it definitely *was* a case. Or three cases, maybe.

First, their new friend Rafael Solares had bought a talkative and noisy parrot from a Mexican man, and Jupiter had hypothesized that the bird had learned his strange collection of sounds on a boat. Where that boat had been docked when it wasn't on the ocean was a question still to be answered – as was the question of how the man had come to own this scarlet macaw in the first place. Also, there was the question of where the bird had learned the phrase, "More capybaras on the way."

Second, when a man named Jack Cutter, who worked in a local bird shop, had overheard the shop owner speaking to Rafael, he had interjected his thoughts about capybaras into a private conversation. Because he had overheard his son Gabriel talking with Cutter on a previous occasion, Rafael had become suspicious, and he wanted The Three Investigators to see what they could find out about Cutter, including whether he had recruited Gabriel into some sort of animal smuggling.

Third, four valuable hyacinth macaws, which had almost certainly been illegally imported into the country, had been discovered in the barn of a man who had never seen them before – a barn from which Jupiter and Pete and Bob had recently seen Slade DeMarco emerging at a time when Wally's son Russell was in the house hanging price tags on his father's furniture.

Although it was just barely possible that Russell didn't know about the macaws in the barn, it was highly improbable. Well, let's face it, Jupiter thought. Impossible.

Although Wally had said, in reference to Slade, that his son was a bad judge of character, when Jupiter remembered Slade's muscle shirt and his biceps, the faint smell of motor oil that hung about him, and the way he'd twirled that gold cross, he thought that Russell might well be a very *good* judge of character when it came to finding someone who could act as a classic enforcer. A good judge of bad character, so to speak.

By now, Jupiter was drowsy, but before he dropped off completely, he managed to do a bit more thinking. Wally had said that Russell had wanted him to move out of his house for quite a while now, and also that he'd been planning to go into business with a Mexican partner. Could the business be the illegal importation of hyacinth macaws, capybaras, and other birds and mammals from South America?

Even though Walter Tate hadn't actually asked anyone to investigate what his son might be up to, he'd made it clear he didn't really trust him, and Jupiter didn't think he'd object if The Three Investigators tried to find out more about him. The story Wally had told them about what Pete had called his haunted thermostat had also lodged in Jupiter's mind as a strange detail, and although he couldn't understand just why at the moment, he thought it was worth looking into further.

So. At least three separate mysteries, as well as three capybaras, four hyacinth macaws, and one Rojo. Why Bob had wanted Mallory to meet the scarlet macaw, Jupiter couldn't imagine, but he *could* imagine Bob would be glad she was back. Even Jupiter wasn't unhappy. After all, the last time he'd seen her had been the night when she and The Three Investigators had finally uncovered the Indian director Madhuri Singh's motives in taking a lot of strange actions at the Rocky Beach Summer Theatre Festival.

Mallory had been great that evening, and after it was over, she'd used a term Jupiter had never heard before to describe what Madhuri Singh had been doing. "It was really almost like gaslighting," she'd said.

Yes, *gaslighting*, thought Jupiter, just as sleep overtook him. Did gaslighting have something to do with this case, too?

6

Into The Inner Sanctum

When Mallory headed off for the Salvage Yard early the next morning, the sun was just beginning to hit the uppermost fronds of the palm trees. The streets were quiet, the air was cool, and automatic sprinklers sent fountains of mist across verdant lawns as people tried to get their watering done before the day got hot.

Even two months after she'd arrived in California from Scotland, Mallory was still amazed at how hard it was to keep the grass green and growing here. In Scotland, everything was green, and it wasn't hard to deduce why Scotland had more sheep than people. If people had been able to eat grass, the situation might have been reversed, she thought, smiling.

As she bicycled along, wearing her recently-purchased but still-unfamiliar bike helmet, Mallory tried to remember just how many sheep (and how many people) Scotland actually had, and although she couldn't be certain, she thought the Scottish sheep population was close to seven million. She would be amazed if California had even a tenth that many sheep —

115

though it had close to forty million people.

Anyway, who cared about all that? she thought. The evening before, she'd gotten an e-mail from Bob Andrews, welcoming her back and filling her in on what had happened with The Three Investigators while she'd been away. This had made her fantastically happy, since while she was gone, she'd missed working at the Salvage Yard, missed The Three Investigators, and even missed Rocky Beach.

Although this had taken her aback, that morning when she'd woken up in her own bed in her own room in Rocky Beach, the first thing she'd done was to look toward the window to see the immigrant's trunk The Three Investigators had given her a few weeks before, sitting snugly under the windowsill. It was still so new that every time she saw it, she had a jolt of pleasure. Nessie, the rubber replica of the Loch Ness monster that she'd won in a contest earlier in the summer, sat atop the chest and fixed Mallory with her little painted eye.

The evening before, when she'd been reading Bob's e-mail she'd also found herself looking at Nessie, and thinking that, all things considered, she'd rather have a rubber Loch Ness monster than a real live scarlet macaw in her house. She didn't like to see birds in cages. Even tame animals should be free, and wild animals should be wild, she thought.

Once, she and her parents had gone on a commercial whale-watching excursion on the Moray Firth when they were visiting Inverness, and they'd seen bottlenose dolphins, harbor porpoises, and pilot and northern bottlenose whales. That day, the wild world had been all around her. The weather had been perfect and the ocean calm. Mallory and her parents had stood up on the right-hand side of the boat, clutching the rail and searching the undulating ocean.

At first, all Mallory had seen was the slowly moving surface of the water. But then it was broken by what seemed to be a long black rock. It rolled and then it flicked its flukes and disappeared.

"It's a pilot whale," her father had said. "There should be a pod of them."

Another whale had surfaced, water spouting from its blowhole, and then another. They sometimes barely broke the surface, but sometimes showed their entire twenty-foot lengths. Mallory had hoped to also see a humpback whale, but they hadn't been lucky enough to spot one. After all, they were very rare there.

In his e-mail, Bob had told Mallory that a man named Rafael Solares had asked The Three Investigators to take care of a parrot named Rojo for a night or two, and that Rojo was currently in Three Investigators Headquarters. Since Mallory had never been invited into this inner sanctum, she wasn't sure how she was going to meet this parrot — which apparently made noises it might have learned from living on a boat. The boys didn't know what boat, or where the boat might be, but they hoped to find out soon.

As Mallory reached the wooden fence surrounding the Jones Salvage Yard, she found herself glancing sideways at an ocean scene. The outside of the fence had been painted with murals crafted by local artists, and this particular section showed a two-masted sailing ship foundering in a raging storm. Bob had shown her that there were two green boards that swung up when you pushed against the eye of a fish looking out of the water at the sinking ship.

Green Gate One was a so-called "secret" entrance to the Salvage Yard, and as Mallory looked at it now, she saw it was ajar. She hit the brakes, jumped off her bike, leaned it against the fence, and adjusted the gate as best she could — though it looked as if it had almost been ripped off its hinges.

At the wrought-iron gates to the Salvage Yard — a pair of large ornate pieces of ironmongery with filigrees and pointed arrows and an arch at the center — she got off her bike again. Although Aunt Mathilda kept the Yard locked after business hours, Mallory had a key, so she opened one of the gates a bit, slipped through with her bike, and locked the gate behind her.

Mallory had never been to the Salvage Yard this early before, and there was no one else around. Leif and Magnus weren't due for at least another hour, and she had no idea when Uncle Titus and Aunt Mathilda usually started working. She parked her bike by the office and began to wander — looking at things that were familiar but which were made new by the unfamiliar circumstances.

In fact, when she found herself in The Three Investigators' outside workshop — where she'd been invited several times — she noticed something she'd never seen before. At one end of the workshop an old oak door, in its frame, stood open. It had always been closed before. In fact, she hadn't known it *could* open, and as she approached to look at it more closely, she saw that it, too, had damage to its hinges — and as she looked through it, she saw, for the first time, an old mobile home which she knew must be The Three Investigators' usually-hidden Headquarters.

Oh, no! Mallory thought. Had someone broken into the Salvage Yard through Green Gate One, then broken into The Three Investigators' office? Walking through the oak door, Mallory was amazed at how beaten up the old mobile home was. It was off its wheels, and its once-shiny metal-plated exterior was dull and dented. The paint on the panels had begun to peel off, and the whole thing was covered with a serious layer of grime. Worst of all, as she got closer, she could see that the door to the mobile home was wide open.

Her sense of propriety kept her from entering without an invitation, so she stood in the doorway and peered inside. It was pretty dark in there with no lights on, but she couldn't see any sign of a colorful red-headed parrot, and although, from what she *could* see, the place hadn't been trashed, as her eyes grew better accustomed to the dimness, she noticed that an office chair she assumed was usually neatly tucked under the desk now lay on its back. It looked as if someone had violently pulled it out in his rush, and it had tipped over and fallen.

Oh my gosh, Mallory thought. There really had been a break-in. She'd better go find Jupiter.

She hurried back across the outdoor workshop and into the main yard. Since the place was still officially closed, and no one was around, there was only one thing to do and that was to walk through the gate at the back of the Yard which led to the house where Jupiter lived with his aunt and uncle.

Aunt Mathilda answered the door. Her hair was tied back with a kerchief and she was wearing an apron. Her face registered surprise and pleasure.

"Good heavens, child," she said. "You're back! What's your hurry? No need to start work this early. We're just finishing breakfast. Would you like to come in for some coffee?"

"No, thank you," Mallory said. "I need to tell Jupiter something."

According to the expression on Aunt Mathilda's face, stranger things had happened. She turned her head and over her shoulder she called in a piercing voice, "Jupiter!" Mallory was sure people heard it in the next county.

In no time at all, Jupiter was standing beside his aunt, and then she smiled and left them alone, after uttering something about getting back to Titus.

"Mallory," Jupiter said. "Is something wrong?"

She was glad to see that he was already dressed, because she knew that as soon as she told him about Bob's e-mail and what she'd found this morning, he'd be off to Headquarters in a flash. And she was right. He walked rapidly past her and led the way to the outdoor workshop. He stopped to examine the old oak door, then turned to her.

"This is Easy Three," he said, "one of the entrances to Headquarters." He went through and into the old mobile home. When she paused in the doorway, Jupiter told her she should come in.

"You might as well," he said.

Mallory was simultaneously amazed that she'd been invited so offhandedly into Headquarters and glad that something so great had happened because of the break-in. When she'd first met The Three Investigators, Jupiter had been the hardest nut to crack. Well, really, he'd been the only nut to crack – Pete and Bob had welcomed her almost right away. But it had taken patience, perseverance, and the lucky break of having been useful in several of their cases this summer for Jupiter to let down his guard.

Even so, who knew how long it would have taken Jupiter to get around to tendering an invitation to Headquarters without this having happened? Another year maybe.

As Mallory watched, he turned on the overhead light and an oscillating fan and got busy checking to see if anything other than Rojo had been taken. As she watched, he also set the desk chair to rights and pushed it firmly under the desk, rifled through the papers on the desktop, checked to make sure that none of the office equipment – an old computer, a printer, a telephone – had been damaged, and then opened a series of drawers to check their contents.

"So far, so good," he said.

While Jupiter continued to check things, Mallory looked more carefully around the interior of Headquarters. It was crowded in there, she thought, and the boys had acted like pretty ordinary boys in their seeming inability to throw anything away. As far as Mallory could see, the shelves and every other available horizontal surface were crammed with stuff. In fact, it looked like everything The Three Investigators had collected since they'd begun their investigative firm was still in Headquarters.

Even so, she was thrilled to see the framed poster she'd given them as a present – CALIFORNIA, CORNUCOPIA TO THE WORLD – displayed prominently on one of the walls. She hadn't seen it since the day they'd given her the immigrant's trunk with her name and the date of her arrival in America painted on it.

Mallory stared at the landline and the old computer and thought that a time-traveler stumbling into this place might not actually know what "now" even meant – not a smartphone in sight, and no tablets or book readers, either. Of course, by now, Mallory had come to understand that the reason for this was the rules laid down by Pete's and Bob's parents and Jupiter's aunt and uncle. Although none of the boys had ever actually said this, it seemed as if they'd almost made deals with their parents in which they'd traded certain kinds of contemporary technology for a lot of genuine freedom.

Although Mallory's parents had never forbidden her from using electronic devices in whatever way she liked, she had somehow – very naturally – found herself using them the same way the boys did. She had an absolute loathing for social media, an aversion to obvious time-wasting, and a deep-seated reluctance to follow the crowd – *any* crowd, she thought. Also, she'd always loved the great outdoors, and when she and her father had gone climbing in the Scottish Highlands, or she'd hiked the John Muir Trail, she'd had a sense she was in touch with something far more important than anything that could be accessed through playing with apps on a smartphone.

Jupiter finished checking the shelves and straightening up. He turned to her, looking both a bit relieved and a bit worried.

"Nothing seems to be missing," he said, "except for a scarlet macaw named Rojo. You said that Bob had sent you an e-mail filling you in? Did he tell you about Rafael Solares? Do you want to sit down?"

He gestured to a folding chair on the other side of the desk, and Mallory briefly wondered whether Bob or Pete usually sat there. As she got as comfortable as she could, Jupiter pulled out the office chair and sat down opposite her.

"It all began two days ago," Jupiter said, and filled her in on the missing pieces of how Rojo had ended up in Headquarters. When he described the yellow truck that had pulled into the Salvage Yard and the man who'd gotten out of it, Mallory was impressed with Jupiter's powers of description. He clearly looked carefully, noticed small details, and filed them away for future reference. She thought his description of Rafael Solares's worry about his son was particularly evocative. By the time he was done, Mallory almost felt as though she'd met the man.

"I guess he'll be upset to discover that Rojo has been stolen," Mallory said.

"Well, maybe," said Jupiter. "But he may also think what you and I do – that the theft of a bird during a break-in has to be seen as a pretty big clue."

Although Mallory found the story Jupiter was telling fascinating, she was having a little trouble concentrating. This was the first time she and he had ever been alone together, and he was talking to her the way he might talk to Pete or Bob. On top of that, he'd just acknowledged that the two of them were alike in the way they looked at the world.

"Yesterday," Jupiter said, "we also met a man named Wally Tate who now lives at the Evergreen Retirement Community but who used to live in the country north of here. He and Rafael were teacher and student at Rocky Beach High, and when we drove to his house with Rafael, we discovered that someone had been keeping four hyacinth macaws in Mr. Tate's barn. Since hyacinth macaws come from the Pantanal in Brazil, can cost over twenty thousand dollars each, and Wally had never seen the birds before, it quickly became clear that we had stumbled on a case of animal smuggling."

Mallory was amazed. She went away for a couple of days and this happened? Parrots were being smuggled into California and there was a break-in at Headquarters? Jupiter looked as focused as she'd ever seen him, and she suddenly felt focused, too.

"Where are the hyacinth macaws now?" she asked curiously.

"With Walter Tate's approval, we took them to our friend Isabella Chang," Jupiter told her. "She's going to take care of them until we can figure out where they should go."

"I guess they can't be sent back to the Pantanal," Mallory mused. "Even if they grew up wild, they might have picked up some sort of infection after they were caught, and they could spread it among the other birds." She wasn't sure why she knew this, but she seemed to remember reading that it was one of the problems with reintroducing animals back into the wild.

"It would also be very expensive, I imagine," Jupiter said. "Anyway, at the moment they're well taken care of – though we can't assume the same about Rojo. I'm afraid the only reasonable explanation for the break-in last night is that whoever smuggled the hyacinth macaws into California somehow figured out that The Three Investigators had been involved in their rescue. He must have come here looking to get them back."

"So you think he got Rojo by accident?" Mallory asked.

"I think when he couldn't find the birds he was actually looking for, he took the one he could get," Jupiter agreed. "The fact that nothing else was taken argues strongly that the thief had birds on his mind and little else."

Mallory kept herself from smiling at this comment. After all, even though to *her* eye, it looked as if a thief would have to be pretty desperate to want to steal anything he might have found in Headquarters, this was hardly the time to make a joke about it.

"Who was the thief, do you think?" she asked instead.

"Just a supposition, but I suspect he was a man named Francis Slade DeMarco. This case started when Pete and Bob and I went out to Walter Tate's place to see some capybaras, and – ”

“Capybaras?” Mallory asked.

“Large South American rodents. Illegal as pets in California. Pete heard from Uncle Titus that he had seen some on a buying expedition, and he wanted to see them, too. When we were on the Tate place, we saw this man named Slade. Early fifties, muscled, brutal. I don't know how he found the Salvage Yard or Headquarters, but I actually think he works for Walter Tate's son, Russell. Walter Tate himself is an admirable man, but his son has crook written all over him. At least to me.”

“Bob and Pete don't agree?” asked Mallory.

“I haven't discussed it with them in any detail yet. They're supposed to be arriving in a little while. In the meantime, I wanted to ask you a question. After Madhuri Singh confessed to Sir Iain, you said ‘It was almost like gaslighting.’ I didn't quite understand what you meant.”

“Well, I'm hardly an expert,” Mallory said, “but I think that classic gaslighting is when you try to make someone think either that they're going crazy, or that something in the world is. What Madhuri Singh did wasn't that exactly, but it was in the ballpark. Why do you ask?"

"Because when we were at Walter Tate's yesterday, Mr. Tate suggested that the major reason he had moved out of his house was because he couldn't get his thermostat to work. He kept getting repair men in, but they couldn't get it fixed. His system was always pumping out hot air on hot days and cold air when it was cold out."

"How odd," Mallory said. "When my mother and I stayed in a motel when we first got to California, there was an electronic thermostat in our room, and we both found it pretty confusing. Maybe Mr. Tate just kept reintroducing the same problem by not knowing what he was doing with the controls."

"Maybe," said Jupiter. "But I'd like to question him further about it. What if someone – like his son Russell – was trying to make his life unbearable? Wouldn't turning the heat on when it was hot out, and the cold when it was cold do that?"

"I guess it would," said Mallory. "And you're right, it would be classic gaslighting. But why would this Russell want his father out of the house?"

Before Jupiter could answer, Mallory heard some voices getting closer. Jupiter had left the door to Headquarters open, and also the door to Easy Three, and now they heard Pete and Bob exclaiming at what they were finding.

"What the – !" Bob said.

"Holy moly," said Pete.

There was the sound of hurried steps and Pete and Bob tumbled into Headquarters.

"Jupe," Pete said. "What's going on? What happened?"

"Mallory!" said Bob, in surprise. "You're in Headquarters!"

"Yes," Jupiter said. "I invited her in. When she got to work this morning, she discovered that someone had broken into Headquarters last night. Rojo is missing."

"Oh no!" Pete said.

"Don't worry, Pete," Jupiter said. "We'll sort this out. I think it's pretty obvious that Slade DeMarco was looking for the hyacinth macaws, and when he couldn't find them, he took Rojo instead."

"Rafael won't blame us," Bob said reassuringly to Pete. "He's not that kind of guy."

"Why don't you both sit down?" Jupiter said. He pointed to a chair. "Pete, that chair from the workshop is still here."

"This is the second time in two days we've had a new person inside Headquarters," Pete explained to Mallory as he sat next to her. "Rafael was in here yesterday. So – " Pete spread his arms wide. " – what do you think?"

Mallory was taken aback, unsure what to say.

Finally she said, "I'm honored to be here. You guys did a great job hiding the place, and I wasn't even sure where it was." Jupiter smiled at this and Pete grinned widely. "But I have to tell you honestly, it won't be showing up in *Better Homes and Gardens* any time soon."

Bob looked puzzled. "What do you mean?" he asked.

"I know it's a guy thing to hold onto stuff, but seriously, have you three ever thrown anything away?" Mallory asked.

Jupiter nodded. "I was thinking myself that it was time for a cleanout."

"With all due respect," Mallory said, "and I sincerely mean that, I think the three of you may have outgrown Headquarters as it is. You've been so successful since you started that maybe it's time to spruce it up. Or maybe even replace it. Plan a Headquarters for who The Three Investigators are now, and then build it. I know you're serious about making a good impression, so you should think about it. It could be really brilliant."

"You mean get rid of this Headquarters and build another one?" Pete asked incredulously.

"Or not," Mallory said.

"She may be right," Bob said. "After all, we've agreed that the place has gotten smaller as we've gotten bigger, and we can't even use Tunnel Two any more. And we haven't used our old Emergency One in forever."

"I used it just this summer," Jupiter said. "Still, there may be something in what Mallory is suggesting. We'll give it a lot of thought. But in the meantime, I'd like to discuss the case, and then, if the three of you are willing, I want to visit Walter Tate again this morning. I have some questions to ask him."

"Shouldn't we call Rafael first?" asked Pete. "We need to tell him that Rojo's been stolen."

"We should certainly call him," said Jupiter. "He may even want to come with us to Wally Tate's again."

"I bet he will," Bob said. "And if we're going to see Wally, maybe we should take the recording I made of Rojo's noises and play it for him. He's owned a lot of birds in his life – a lot of parrots – and I keep thinking there's something about the noises we're missing."

"The scarlet macaw made noises?" Mallory asked.

"Oh, boy, did he ever," Pete said. "He made a noise like a motor, and one like a siren, and one that sounded like wind and waves. Jupe thinks he must have lived on a boat somewhere. He also said 'More capybaras on the way'."

"Why would a bird say *that*?" Mallory said.

"That's one of the things we need to discover," Jupiter said. "Why don't you call Rafael, Bob? You have his number stored in your phone. And Pete, see if you can get the hinges fixed on Easy Three. Mallory, if you want to come with us to visit Walter Tate, you'd be quite welcome, but you should probably tell Aunt Mathilda that you won't be working this morning, after all."

Suddenly, all was bustle, and after Bob took out his phone to call Rafael Solares, in very short order everyone was sitting on the porch of the Salvage Yard office waiting for him to pick them up and take them to the Evergreen Retirement Community. Rafael had been shocked to hear about the theft of the scarlet macaw, but, as Bob had expected, he'd been sympathetic rather than upset.

Aunt Mathilda had seemed disappointed that Mallory had arrived only to leave again, but by this time, Mallory felt confident enough in her job that she knew she'd be forgiven for *that*. What she'd been a little more worried about was the way Pete had reacted to her suggestion that it might be time for a new Three Investigators Headquarters. Jupiter hadn't seemed all that thrilled, either, she thought.

Bob, of course, had been really nice about it, but until Jupiter had invited her to join them on this visit to Walter Tate's, she'd been worried she might have blotted her copybook with the whole gang. She was very relieved to learn she hadn't, and as she sat and waited for Rafael Solares, she found herself wondering whether 'blotting your copybook' was an idiom in America as well as in Scotland.

Probably not, she concluded. However, since she couldn't be certain, she turned to Bob and asked.

7

A Perfect Prodigy

Bob had been sitting quietly, waiting for Rafael to arrive, so he was surprised by Mallory's sudden question. Ever since he'd gotten to the Salvage Yard that morning, he'd been feeling both exhilarated and confused. He was happy Mallory was back in Rocky Beach and delighted to find that Jupiter had invited her into Headquarters, but at the same time worried that someone brazen enough to break into the Salvage Yard and then Headquarters could be a pretty violent man.

At Bob's feet was his backpack with his laptop and digital recorder inside, and he'd been wondering whether to play the recording of Rojo on his headphones, just in case something about it triggered a thought, when Mallory turned to him and said, "Do people blot copybooks in America?"

At first, Bob thought Mallory had said "capybaras" but even when he got that the word was "copybooks" he had no idea what Mallory was talking about. Until she added, "As an idiom, I mean."

"Oh, you mean do we say that so and so has blotted his copybook – meaning made a mess of things?" he asked.

"Yes," said Mallory, nodding. "I think it goes back to when people used fountain pens filled from an ink bottle."

"I've read the saying in English novels," Bob said, "but I don't think I've ever heard anyone use it in conversation."

He was going to ask her why she'd thought of it when Rafael's bright yellow pickup appeared.

Pete and Jupiter both jumped to their feet. Bob and Mallory rose a little more slowly, then followed Jupiter who introduced her to Rafael. When she asked how long he'd be staying in Rocky Beach, he said he was leaving that afternoon to head back to his house in Isla Vista.

"Isla Vista?" Mallory asked. "Where's that?"

"Northwest of Santa Barbara," said Rafael. "It's got a population of about twenty-three thousand. A lot of students from UC Santa Barbara and a lot of working class Hispanics. I live in a house right on the ocean. It's very small, and perched on a cliff that may wash away one of these days, but at the moment it's still standing – covered with dark brown weather-beaten shingles, and with a tiny yard."

"It sounds great," Mallory said. "Do you ever get out on the ocean?"

"Quite often," Rafael said. "I have a boat called *The Rainbow Bridge*. I bought it from a guy who used to run whale-watching expeditions in the Channel Islands. It's shabby, but it works."

"*The Rainbow Bridge*," asked Bob. "As in the Chumash origin myth?"

"The very same," Rafael said smiling, "A nod to that half of my ancestry – and also the mystical part of my nature. Well, are you guys ready to go see Wally again? I told him we'd be there soon."

Yesterday, coming back from Walter Tate's place in the country, Wally and Jupiter had ridden in front with Rafael, but now Pete claimed the honor. So Bob, Jupiter, and Mallory climbed in the back and made themselves comfortable for the ten-minute ride to Evergreen.

On the way, Jupiter seemed eager to continue a conversation he'd apparently been having with Mallory before Bob and Pete had arrived at the Salvage Yard.

"I don't know if Bob noticed," he said to her, "but when Walter Tate discovered that almost every piece of furniture in his house had a price tag on it, he told Rafael he couldn't remember whether or not he'd told Russell he could sell whatever he wanted."

"I did notice," Bob said. "I thought he didn't want to admit that his son had gone behind his back."

"I thought that, too," Jupiter said, "and I was just saying to Mallory that I thought Wally's story about his haunted thermostat was quite intriguing. I want to ask him more about his son."

Bob had liked Walter Tate the minute he met him, and when he thought about the possibility that Russell was using his father − for his money or his place or something else − he felt quite angry. Jupiter might want to quiz Wally about Russell, but he, Bob, wanted to hear him tell more stories about his life. The repartee he and Isabella had engaged in had been truly dazzling, Bob thought. He also didn't think it was an accident that thirty years after he'd first heard them, Rafael remembered the details of Wally's war stories.

He was a man who loved language − who would have known at once what the phrase 'blotting your copybook' meant. He had a facility for easy and quick conversation, a dry sense of humor, and an expansive acceptance of the situation he found himself in. Bob hoped he was half as sharp if he ever reached Wally Tate's age.

Soon they were pulling up to Evergreen – a name that Bob suspected Wally must find a little irritating. In the parking lot, Rafael told them that when he'd called, Wally had said he'd meet them in the outside gardens.

Jupiter said he was eager to pass on a message from Isabella Chang.

"What message?" asked Pete curiously.

"Before Mallory arrived this morning, Isabella called to say that she'd decided to move the hyacinth macaws into the spare wing of her house. She showed it to us the night we had dinner with her."

"That's right!" Pete said. "She told us an old friend of hers had lived with her until she died."

"The point is, it's empty now," Jupiter said, "and this morning, Isabella and Charlotte are going to move the birds off her dining table and into the empty rooms. She asked if we were going to be seeing Wally again, and when I said we had no plans to at the moment, she said, 'Well, if you do, tell him he's welcome to come visit me anytime. In fact, if he wants to move into the wing when the birds move out, I'd love to have him!' She seemed to mean it," Jupiter said.

"Yikes!" said Pete. "That was fast! I guess when you get to that age, you don't want to waste time with small talk. And it's a terrific idea, really. Isabella and Wally have a lot in common, and if Jupiter wants to grill Wally about Russell, it'll be nice to be able to give him some good news at the same time."

"I don't plan to 'grill' him at all," Jupiter said, "but since I hope to ask him a few questions, I thought maybe you could relay Isabella's invitation first."

"I like the sound of this," Rafael said. "By the way," he asked Mallory, "what's your role in this enterprise?"

Bob could tell this made Mallory uncomfortable, so he jumped into action. "We just met Mallory about two months ago, but she's been terrific," he said. "I can't tell you how much she's helped us out. She's been crucial to the solutions of three out of four cases so far this summer."

Mallory looked at him gratefully and he smiled at her. Then Rafael led the way to the outdoor gardens where the first thing Bob saw was Walter Tate, sitting on a bench next to a small manmade pond. Jupiter introduced him to Mallory, and once the five of them had found seats around him, Wally asked what they'd been up to and whether they'd heard anything from Isabella Chang.

Since Jupiter had appointed Pete as the bearer of good news, Pete did his best to convey Isabella's playful invitation in the proper way. But when Wally simply sat and stared at him, Pete looked dismayed.

"There's a sudden roaring in my ears," Wally said. "Could you say that again?"

Pete cleared his throat. "Ms. Chang told Jupiter that if we saw you we should tell you that she really enjoyed meeting you and that you can visit her any time."

"That's not what you said before," Wally said. "I told you I had a sudden roaring in my ears, not that I'd gone deaf."

Pete smiled. "She also said there's a whole spare wing in her house if you wanted to move in with her. And you should think about it!" Pete added. "You could keep each other company."

Wally smiled slyly. "Young man," he said, "I know a thing or two about keeping company. Even so, I can hardly believe it. That heavenly creature asked me to come and stay with her? I feel I've undergone a – dare I say it? – a metamorphosis. I was a caterpillar and now I'm a butterfly! A thinking butterfly. Thinking hard. What do *you* think, Rafael?"

"I think my old friend has landed on his feet," Rafael said. "Or, more accurately, taken wing. There's an old Chumash saying that birds of a feather flock together."

"That can't *really* be a Chumash saying!" Pete exclaimed.

"It might be," Rafael said, smiling. "My mother used to say it." To Wally, he said, "You seemed a little discouraged when we got here. Has anything happened since yesterday afternoon?"

Wally looked grim. "Last night Russell stopped by, unannounced and unexpected. He pretended he'd just come for a visit, but by then, between one thing and another, I had reason to take his explanation with a pinch of salt. So when he asked me offhandedly if I'd been out to the house, I feigned surprise and said no. I asked if there was anything the matter, and Russell said he'd just been out there and had found five water glasses in the sink."

"Did he mention the macaws?" asked

Jupiter.

"He did not," Wally responded. "Nor did I."

He grimaced, then turned to Jupiter. "After he left, I noticed that your business card was missing from the table where I'd set it down, and ever since Rafael called this morning and told me there had been a break-in at your Salvage Yard, I've been worried that I was its cause. Or not me, but my progeny and my carelessness combined."

"You can't be held responsible for the actions of your son," Jupiter said. "And I'm actually quite relieved to know how we were tracked down. Since I didn't tell the truth when your son asked who my uncle was – and Slade DeMarco wasn't even interested in asking – I could only imagine that one or the other of them had noted the license plate of the Salvage Yard truck when we were out looking at the capybaras. But since there was no real reason for either Russell or Slade to be suspicious until *after* the hyacinth macaws went missing, I found it hard to convince myself they'd been so eagle-eyed."

"But *you* would have been that eagle-eyed," Wally said to Jupiter.

"He sure would!" said Pete. "In fact,

we're having a new logo designed for our firm – a chimera, with three heads – and Jupe is the golden eagle!"

Wally looked at Pete, Bob, and Jupiter keenly. "A chimera!" he said admiringly. "I find that reassuring, from a pedagogical point of view. However, I'm very distressed at the strong possibility that my son and his disreputable friend are smuggling endangered birds into California."

There was little that anyone could say to this except what Jupiter *did* say. "If they are, we'll try to put a stop to it. Rafael has asked us to start by investigating a man named Jack Cutter who works at Veronica's Exotic Birds."

"I know," said Wally. "Rafael told me he thought he might have gotten his hooks into Gabriel. I remember him from my trips to Veronica's to buy cockatiels and cockatoos and so on and so forth. Although he liked to be called 'Cutter,' he never struck me as a particularly suspicious character."

"When I was talking to Veronica about Rojo's remark about capybaras, he came over to say he thought capybaras should be legal in California," Rafael said.

"So they should be!" said Wally. "And as I seem to remember, you concur! But what's all this about capybaras? You told me a scarlet macaw had been stolen last night, but you never told me he'd been talking about capybaras!"

"Do you want to hear him?" Bob asked suddenly. "Before he was stolen, I made a recording. He makes a noise like a motor and a noise like a siren and a noise that sounds like the creaking of a boat. And he also makes a noise that sounds like some strange kind of music."

"What does he say about capybaras?" asked Wally.

"He says,'More capybaras on the way'!" Pete exclaimed.

"He sounds like a prodigy," Wally remarked. He nodded to Bob, who had taken the recorder out of his pocket. When Bob hit the PLAY button, Rojo's performance filled the garden at Evergreen with sounds that ranged from the interesting to the irritating. The comment about capybaras was repeated several times, as were the whooshing and creaking, and the motor straining to start.

When the recording arrived at the section where the bird started making noises that sounded to Bob like music, both Wally and Mallory leaned forward intently. Mallory seemed particularly interested in the series of notes that rose in sequence, one after the other, then fell.

When the recording was over, Mallory asked Bob, "Can you play that last part again?" When he had, she said, with total conviction, "That's a carillon."

"A what?" Pete asked.

"A carillon," Mallory said. "An arrangement of at least twenty-three bells. You play it at a keyboard like a piano, and hammers strike the bells and make them ring. You can play whole melodies. Mostly they're found in churches. They have one at Dumferline Abbey, near where I used to live in Scotland."

"The girl is right," Wally said. "They have a number of them in France, and when I was there learning how to hobble around on shrapnel, I had the pleasure of hearing one in the cathedral at Rouen. What's the one at Dumferline like?" he asked Mallory.

"Loud," Mallory said. "Dumferline is actually an ancient Benedictine abbey, but its first bells weren't installed until just before the Second World War. The largest bell in the carillon weighs more than half a ton. I've always wondered how on earth they installed it into a bell tower!"

"I've never heard of carillons," Bob said. "But if they're an Old World invention, maybe some of the Spanish missions have them."

"That's an interesting suggestion," Jupiter said. "Maybe in a little while you can get onto your laptop and see if you can find a list of carillons in Mexico or California. But first I want to ask Mr. Tate – Wally – something."

Turning to Wally, Jupiter said, "When we were out at your house, you told us your thermostat had been acting up, and I'm hoping you can tell me more about it. I know it sounds odd, but I have a reason for asking."

"Shoot," Wally said. "Or don't shoot. But ask away."

"Since your house is quite old, and the electronic thermostat is modern, I'm wondering whether your whole system was replaced when the thermostat was replaced, or whether you just gave an old system a modern set of controls."

"The latter," said Wally. "We used to have a mechanical thermostat with a switch that let me put it on either Heating or Cooling. I could set the temperature simply by sliding a mechanical bar. It was very reliable – in fact, it never failed. But three years ago, Russell and Cynthia convinced me and Patricia it was time to get modern and put in a self-adjusting thermostat. At first, we thought it was great. We never had to touch it. About a year and a half ago, all that changed."

"I see," Jupiter said. "Did you ever talk to your children about the problem?"

"Did we ever!" said Wally. "As I told you, Cynthia thought it was a sign from the Great Spirit that it was time for us to move somewhere else. Russell was more reasonable, but every time he came to the house to work on the controls, he suggested that I must be changing them and then forgetting I had done so. It was bad enough to have the house always be the wrong temperature, but I didn't appreciate being told I was going crazy. I finally asked Russell to find me a good old-fashioned thermostat − like the one we'd had for thirty years − but he said they weren't making them any more."

When he heard this, Bob felt even more upset on Wally's behalf, but Jupiter seemed satisfied and suggested it was time to leave. Since Wally no longer had his original Three Investigators card, Bob pulled one from his wallet and put it into Wally's hand.

"If you ever need to call us for any reason, please do," he said.

"I will, my boy," Wally said. "And thank you."

"So do you want me to look up carillons now?" Bob asked Jupiter.

"Yes," he said. "Let's see what we can find out. If we're right that Rojo recently lived on a boat, and we can find a place in California where there's a carillon and a marina close to one another, we may be able to go there and investigate the matter for ourselves."

Bob grabbed his backpack, pulled his laptop out, and asked Wally if Evergreen had a password for its Wi-Fi.

"If it does, my boy, then I surely don't know what it is," said Wally, grinning broadly.

Luckily, no password was required, so Bob positioned his laptop in such a way that he could see the screen even in the sunshine. When he typed "carillons in southern California" into the search box, he found a link to a page that listed not only the carillons in southern California, but all the carillons in the entire world.

As it turned out, there were a lot of them. There were sixty-four carillons in the tiny region of Flanders alone. Over a thousand carillons were listed on the page, but only a single one was in Mexico — in Mexico City, which Bob knew wasn't on the ocean. There were a mere handful in California — almost all of them on university campuses, not in Spanish missions. If Jupe's hypothesis was right, none of those would work, since Rojo would have had to be in a marina when he learned the carillon's sounds.

So Bob was intrigued to discover that there *were* a few pseudo-carillons — an electronic instrument that imitated the sounds of a carillon and amplified them through loudspeakers — installed here and there in California. It wasn't as easy to get information about them as it was about real carillons, but after a lot of digging around, Bob discovered that a pseudo-carillon had been installed in a small Catholic church called St. Peter's-by-the-Sea about five years before.

"Holy mackerel," Bob said to the others. "You're not going to believe this but one of the few carillons in California is actually in Isla Vista. Well, not a carillon but something called a pseudo-carillon. It doesn't have actual bells. It's some sort of electronic instrument. It's in a church called St. Peter's-by-the-Sea."

"St. Peter's-by-the-Sea?" said Rafael, surprised. "I think I've seen it. I may even have been there once. But I don't remember ever hearing any carillon."

"Are there any details about the melodies the carillon plays?" Jupiter asked intently.

"Not that I can find," said Bob. "And the telephone number they're listing is only good on Sundays. Plus, although there's an address, I don't know how far the building is from the sea."

"It's pretty close," Rafael said. "And unless I'm much mistaken, it's – well, why don't you pull up a map, and see?"

Bob did that, and the map not only showed that St. Peter's was less than a block from the ocean but the same distance from a fair-sized marina – almost certainly the marina in which Rojo had been perched when he learned his amazing repertoire of sounds, and therefore almost certainly a marina in which animal smuggling was taking place.

Rafael smiled grimly.

"Just as I thought," he said. "How do the four of you feel about coming to Isla Vista tomorrow to do some investigating on my home turf?"

8

To The Rainbow Bridge

The following day, Jupiter, Pete, and Bob were packing their camping gear in the Salvage Yard. A lot had happened in a very short time, Jupiter thought. Worthington would soon be arriving to drive the three of them — and Mallory — up to Rafael Solares's house, where he'd invited them to pitch a tent in his back yard for a day or two.

Isla Vista was only an hour and a half from Rocky Beach, but some further research on Bob's part had determined that the carillon only rang out once a day, at 5:00.

While Jupiter supposed that it wasn't *totally* necessary for The Three Investigators to hear the sound of it for themselves, they still all wanted to do that — and they didn't want to have to race right back to Rocky Beach afterwards, especially because the real reason they were going to Isla Vista was to check out the marina next to the church.

Luckily, Worthington was available to drive them — though he had other trips to make that day and could only take them just past

153

noon.

Pete and Bob and even Mallory had had no trouble getting permission to go, and all Aunt Mathilda had said to Jupiter was "Bring extra socks!"

Now they were packing to leave. They'd gotten their equipment from the shed where they stored it and were going over their gear. Their sleeping bags still held the smell of wood smoke from the camping trip they'd taken to Yosemite earlier that summer, and they were airing them in the sun while they unfolded their big tent, refolded it neatly, and then did the same for the smaller tent they were bringing for Mallory.

Jupiter had made sure they had their walkie-talkies. Luckily there were four of those – one for each of them and an extra one for Mallory. They'd bought new walkie-talkies at the beginning of the summer, and although these were supposed to have a range of fifty miles, the furthest they'd ever been able to test them was about thirty miles.

Anyway, they certainly didn't expect to get separated. The batteries were fully charged, and Jupiter made sure they were all on the same frequency.

It was fun to be packing for another

camping trip − even one that was just in someone's backyard − and since Jupiter had called
Isabella Chang the night before, and she had
reassured him that the hyacinth macaws were
fine, he would have been feeling almost care-
free if it hadn't been for a piece of information
he'd gotten that morning.

After parking his bike and pulling off his
backpack, Bob had come over to Jupiter with
an intense look in his eyes. "Jupe, remember
what Wally Tate told us Russell said about his
old-fashioned thermostat? I got online last
night − I don't even know why − and I found
two different companies still making the kind of
thermostat with the On and Off switch for
Heat and Cold, and the bar you can slide
along until it reaches the temperature you
want. They were cheap, too. Less than
$50.00."

"So you think Russell was lying?" Jupiter
asked.

"Well, I guess he could just be really bad
at looking for stuff on the Internet, but I think
he could have found them if he'd tried."

Bob had looked quite concerned, and
ever since, Jupiter had been pondering the
situation. Although he was proud of Bob for
having looked into the matter further, Jupiter

almost wished he hadn't.

There was a phrase – 'the ghost in the machine' – that Jupiter had run into, and although he had the impression that it meant something more complex than it seemed to, it came into his mind as he sorted through his gear.

If Russell had really wanted to get his father out of his house, for some reason yet to be determined, what better way than to make the house unbearable to live in? From Russell's point of view, a side benefit of putting a ghost in the machine would be to try to make his father think he was going crazy.

While this hypothesis made sense to Jupiter, he couldn't think of any easy way for Russell to have hacked the thermostat, and he decided to put it out of his mind by reviewing the events of the afternoon before.

Rafael had dropped them off at the Salvage Yard before taking off for Santa Barbara where he had some sort of meeting of special education teachers he needed to attend. Pete, Bob and Jupiter had bicycled all the way to Veronica's Exotic Birds to see if they could meet Jack Cutter – or find out something more about him.

But when they got there, it turned out

he'd taken the whole week off. He'd had a number of personal days coming to him and had decided to take them now.

The Three Investigators had, however, learned that Jack Cutter had been hired by Veronica Harrison quite a while ago; that he was a genuine animal lover; that the only strange thing about his working at her shop was that when he'd started, he hadn't known much about birds; and that at home he had four dogs, three cats, and a turtle. Veronica had also told The Three Investigators that Jack Cutter had been doing more and more of her paperwork.

"Hey, Jupe," Pete called out to him. "What about food? Should we take some of our freeze-dried stuff, and nuts and raisins and crackers, just in case?"

Bob laughed. "We're not going to Antarctica. Just an hour and a half away, to a city of 23,000 people − and a lot of stores!"

"Yeah, I know," Pete said, sounding slightly aggrieved. "But it can't hurt to be prepared."

"That's true," Jupiter said. "I don't think the freeze-dried food will be needed this time, but there's no reason why we shouldn't bring nuts and raisins."

"Great!" Pete said, stuffing bags of both into his pack.

Their gear was stacked and ready on the office porch, and Mallory had just arrived by bike – her backpack full, her sleeping bag slung underneath it – when Worthington pulled up and parked his car beside the Flex. He climbed out and said hello, then opened the hatchback and started loading it with their gear.

Jupiter hadn't seen Worthington since the case at the Rocky Beach Theatre Festival had wrapped up, and he was happy he was here. Mallory got in front with Worthington, and the three boys jumped in the back.

There was some jostling to determine who had to ride in the middle, and as usual it wound up being Bob – who was so good-natured about it that Jupiter thought of changing places with him. But just for a minute. Soon they were speeding north, close to the coast.

"So what's this new case all about?" Worthington asked as he drove.

There was a lot to tell, but Jupiter filled him in as best he could. Worthington was shocked to hear about the break-in at Headquarters and the theft of the scarlet macaw, but for some reason Jupiter's obsessive mind kept circling back to the thermostat. Pete might have been satisfied with thinking the device was "haunted," but Jupiter wanted to know what was really going on.

"Worthington," he asked. "Do you know anything about thermostats?"

"Thank god for them," Worthington said. "Clever devices. Perhaps not so important for parts of California, but back in the U.K., let me tell you, no one takes central heating for granted."

Mallory laughed at this. "I don't think I even knew what *warm* meant until we moved to Rocky Beach," she said.

"What do you want to know?" Worthington said. "If you think I might understand how they work, you'd be wrong."

"We have a friend," Jupiter told him, "whose thermostat seems to have gone haywire. When it's hot out, the thermostat tells the furnace to heat the house, and when it's cold, the air conditioning comes on."

"Clearly it's broken," Worthington said, "but surely you didn't need me to tell you that. Perhaps your friend should replace it with one like mine. I find it ever so convenient."

"How?" Jupiter said.

"It's what they call a 'smart' thermostat," Worthington said. "I don't even have to be in the house to control it. I have an application on my phone that lets me set the temperature from wherever I am, and since I'm away from the house a lot, that's a real bonus."

Jupiter didn't have a smartphone and had never really examined one; he knew they weren't exactly play toys, and he supposed that once he acquired one, he would appreciate certain of their features, but at the moment he had the impression that they were a huge waste of time for anyone who owned one. Still, not having a smartphone put him at a disadvantage when it came to understanding what most people thought of as one of the wonders of the modern age.

"This application lets you raise and lower the temperature at will?" Jupiter asked. "Could you turn the air conditioning on from here?"

"Absolutely," Worthington said. "It's both useful and sensible for a single man like myself. I rarely know when I'll be getting back home, so it's convenient to be able to keep the heat or air from pumping unnecessarily when I'm not there. About an hour before I return, I reset the temperature so it will be comfortable when I get home."

"Wow!" Pete said. "What are they going

to think of next?"

"I hesitate to imagine," Jupiter said. He turned back to Worthington. "And I presume that you and only you can do this?"

"Yes," Worthington said. "The application on my phone is tied to my account with the company that makes the thermostat."

"Ingenious," Jupiter said.

Ingenious was one word for it, he thought, but diabolical was another. From what Worthington had just told him, it seemed entirely possible that Russell Tate had linked his phone to the thermostat in Wally's house, and that, no matter where Wally might set it, Russell could override and reset it to make his father as uncomfortable as possible.

It suddenly struck Jupiter as not only possible but almost a certainty – a plan so devious no one would ever guess, and one that might have caused a man less strong than Wally to fear that he was losing his sanity.

As it was, all it had done was create the conditions under which it seemed wise to move out of his own home. But if Russell Tate had figured out a way to control the temperature in his father's house, what else about his father's life was he controlling? Jupiter pinched his lip, hard. This would take some looking into.

In the front seat, Mallory had been listening to the conversation between Jupiter and Worthington with real interest – and not just because she was interested in the topic, but also because she was interested in the way Jupiter's mind worked. The way he took a problem that seemed to have no solution and worried it until a solution suggested itself. After all, she frequently did the same herself. It was one of the things that set her apart from a lot of her fellow teenagers – and particularly from a lot of her fellow girls, she thought wryly.

Bob had recently lent her a book called *Darwin's Moral Mammals*, and the section on the biological differences between males and females had really made her think. One chapter had reviewed the fact that, when it came to certain traits, there was more variation among the male sex than the female. This had come about as a result of natural selection, generally held true across the animal kingdom, and had first been noted by Charles Darwin in his book *The Descent of Man*.

The thing that had interested Mallory the most was that it seemed to apply to human intelligence – that when you looked at scores in intelligence tests, there were more males than females at either end of the statistical distribution curve – more male geniuses and more male idiots.

There seemed to be no doubt about this; the book cited the fact that among the people scoring in the top two per cent of America's Armed Forces Qualification Test, men outnumbered women by a ratio of almost 2 to 1. Of course, this didn't mean that there weren't plenty of female geniuses and plenty of female idiots – just that there were a few more of each when it came to the male of the species.

Mallory had read the explanation about why, exactly, this had happened, in evolutionary terms, but at the moment she wasn't thinking about that explanation. Since she had never had any doubts about her own intelligence, she didn't feel threatened by the indisputable scientific fact that there were more males than females in her cohort; she knew she could hold her own with anyone, when it came to the matter of intelligence.

No, what she was thinking about at the moment was something else. You'd never know from listening to Jupiter talk to Worthington that, in making no objection to Rafael's off-the-cuff suggestion that she accompany The Three

Investigators on this adventure, Jupiter had been moving into unknown territory.

There she was, sitting in the front seat of a car he and his friends had bought as a vehicle for their investigative firm, and although, just two months ago, Jupiter would clearly never have imagined that he would be inviting *anyone* to come with him and the others on a trip like this, here she was.

It was really great, Mallory thought – especially because although she'd been with the boys on a number of important occasions, she hadn't yet had a chance to just kick back with all three of them at the same time. While she'd liked the time she'd spent with Bob – somehow, up to the present, it had been mostly Bob she'd spent extra time with – she was really looking forward to hanging out with all of them at once, the way she had with her closest friends in Scotland.

Back there, she'd had friends of both sexes and had liked each of them in a different way, but the truth was, she'd always found boys more challenging – and had liked the kind of challenge they posed. With boys, you had to be on your toes all the time. She thought fleetingly of second grade, and how boys had shrieked in terror over the possibility that girls would give them cooties, and although Jupiter certainly didn't think that, he also didn't believe in unnecessary intimacy.

That was why it had been such a satisfaction – and even a triumph – when he had invited her into Three Investigators Headquarters for the first time. Somehow, he had judged that intimacy necessary – which meant he had judged her necessary, at least at that moment. Whether he would keep doing that or not remained to be seen, she thought – but in order to maximize the chances, she planned to keep being as useful and clever as she could.

About halfway to Isla Vista, Worthington stopped at a diner where they ate lunch. After coffee and lemon meringue pie, they climbed back into the car and finished the trip to Rafael Solares's house. When Worthington pulled up, everyone clambered out, but before they could get to the door, Rafael came through it.

Once again, his hair was pulled back into a ponytail but today it was fastened with scarlet twine. The small weather-beaten house with dark brown shingles and a jutting porch stood on a bluff that overlooked the Pacific – one in a crowded row of similar houses separated by ramshackle wooden or wire fences, crowded together but wide open to the water.

It was an amazing place, Mallory thought – thirty feet above the surf as it crashed at the rocks at the foot of the bluff. The ocean looked vast and wind-tossed and glittery, like the North Sea but strewn with light. Mallory and the others went back to the Flex and thanked Worthington, then stood and waved until he was out of sight.

The house was simple, but Mallory could see that every object and piece of furniture had been chosen with care. There were a number of carvings of sea animals, including a carving of a whale. There were also lots of books.

Rafael offered them coffee, and they all said yes. As he was pouring it into a set of colorful mugs, Rafael surprised Mallory by saying that his girlfriend Elena, with whom he lived, had grown up not far from St. Peter's and could remember when the carillon had been installed. At one time it had played twice daily – at noon and at five in the evening – but recently the parish had decided to save money on electricity by reducing its use to just once a day.

"It'll be good to hear it and confirm that it is, in fact, the same carillon that Rojo must have heard," Jupiter said, "but of course the real reason we're here is to investigate the marina where he must have heard it. We need to look for a boat that might be smuggling capybaras from Mexico to California."

"And not just capybaras," said Bob. "Possibly also scarlet and hyacinth macaws."

"That's right," said Rafael. "Which would be far, far worse. And the more I think about it, the more I doubt it was a coincidence that we found four hyacinth macaws in Wally's barn. If Jack Cutter *has* recruited Gabriel into some sort of animal smuggling that uses Veronica's Exotic Birds as a cover, he might have found it easier to convince my son that there was nothing really wrong with what they were doing if Russell Tate was involved, too. After all, ever since Gabriel was really small, he's known both Wally and Russell. And Russell used to like to play a game where he tossed Gabriel into the air."

"I see what you mean," said Jupiter.

"Anyway," Rafael said, "since it's going to be several hours before we can go to St. Peter's and hear the carillon, maybe I should take the four of you for a ride in my boat. A week or two ago, when I was fishing not far from the lighthouse on Point Conception, I noticed three sailboats close together. Something about the way they were idling made it look as if they were waiting for someone else.

"I don't know why they would have done that," Rafael went on, "but there are landing spots up and down the coast which smugglers have used as rendezvous points. Now that we know that there's a very good chance that whoever originally owned Rojo kept him on board a sailboat regularly moored in the marina a block from St. Peter's, it also seems likely that he was bringing capybaras up the coast from South America. Of course, they might have been offloaded almost anywhere in the basic region of Isla Vista, but even so, I'd like to take the boat out and see what we can see."

"That sounds great," said Pete. "Because *I'd* like to see what we can see, anyway! It's been a long time since we had a case that took us to the ocean. Maybe we'll see some sea otters. I really think they're the cutest animals in the world."

"I agree," said Rafael, "and it's sad to think that the coastal Chumash once killed them both for their meat and for their coats. They also traded sea otter meat and fur with the Chumash who lived inland."

"What else did they trade?" asked Jupiter.

"Seal pelts and swordfish and whale meat and oil," Rafael said. "They had boats called plank canoes strong enough so that they could hunt whales. The inland Chumash traded venison and acorns and stuff like that. Of course, when the Europeans arrived, everything changed"

Mallory was impressed with how straightforward and even pragmatic Rafael was about Chumash history. Even though he was the direct descendant of a people who had started to be romanticized after most of them had died, he himself didn't want to romanticize them. There was a lesson in there somewhere, Mallory thought – and not just in general, but for her. Though right at the moment, she wasn't sure quite what it was.

"All right, then," said Rafael. "Let's go. You might want to bring your backpacks." As he led the way outside, and as the others grabbed their gear, Mallory thought of disattaching her sleeping bag but then decided it would take too long and just tossed her backpack into the back of Rafael's hand-painted yellow truck. At Rafael's invitation, she and Jupiter got into the front. Jupiter sat in the middle of the platform seat, next to Rafael, while Mallory sat by the door with the window open.

It seemed there were two marinas in Isla Vista, and it took just five minutes to get to the one where Rafael kept his boat. After he'd parked, and they'd all grabbed their backpacks, the four of them followed him down the pier and onto the deck of *The Rainbow Bridge.*

It looked a lot like the boat on which she'd gone whale-watching with her parents – thirty-five or forty feet long, with twin outboard motors on the back and a canopied area in front of them which housed the driver and the wheel. The boat had an inflated rubberized rim and could probably have taken fifteen people. Luckily, there were just five of them.

Rafael fitted them all with life jackets, and they settled themselves and their gear on seats in the rear of the boat, near where Rafael held the wheel. Soon they were flying over the waves, heading north, toward the lighthouse on Point Conception – though Rafael said that the water was too rough for them to go all the way today.

Even so, as she stood looking out at the sea, Mallory felt as happy as she had since her father's death. The air smelled of salt and ozone, and the coast to their right, with its cliffs and rocky beaches, coves and inlets, shone brilliantly in the afternoon sun. Seagulls circled lazily overhead as the *Rainbow Bridge* sped north, the ocean's waves thudding against the hull as the yacht jumped along like a porpoise. Far out in the ocean to the west, Rafael pointed out a pod of pilot whales breaking the surface.

Then he suddenly slowed the boat and pointed to something much closer at hand. Mallory saw a raft of sea otters, the mothers drifting on their backs holding their pups close, all of them seemingly tangled in kelp. They looked up placidly and wiggled their whiskers. Even though Mallory didn't think of herself as overly susceptible to the charms of animals in general, these sea otters lying on their backs, scratching their chests and grabbing their cheeks with their paws made her almost feel giddy. Yes, she really *was* happy, she suddenly realized.

And while she was sure she would always miss Scotland and her father, maybe *this* was the lesson she'd been reaching for earlier that afternoon. That although there's a lot of sadness in life, and you have to feel grief when it happens, if and when things get better, you don't need to keep dwelling on what's past.

She looked at Pete and Bob, who were keeping their balance as the *Rainbow Bridge* thudded over the waves. Pete had his eyes on the ocean and was taking deep breaths of the salt air, while Bob was watching Rafael steer – and while Mallory had actually been a little worried that if she accepted Rafael's invitation to accompany The Three Investigators to Isla Vista, she really *would* end up blotting her copybook with them, so far, at least, it hadn't happened. It was amazing what could happen in life if you just kept moving forward, she reflected. She was out on the open ocean with Jupiter, Pete, and Bob – and in the midst of a real investigation!

9

Seeing Double

Not far from where Mallory was standing, Pete was watching the pilot whales, but still thinking about the sea otters they'd just passed. Lying on their backs, paws together, as though the great wide ocean was their own personal bathtub, they'd looked up at him as if they were seeing him for who he really was. They looked so incredibly *innocent* that it was hard to believe that anyone, anywhere, had ever killed them for their fur or their meat.

But, of course, it was stupid to think that, Pete thought. When it came to staying warm or fed, the Chumash had done what they had to do – just as people everywhere had always had to. Killing animals like sea otters for their fur and meat in the old days wasn't at all the same as killing wild elephants for their tusks, rhinoceroses for their horns, or tigers for their claws, bones, and teeth. On the way up to Isla Vista, Bob had been telling him that there were still people who did that, as well as people who killed sharks for their fins – and just to make a soup.

173

Pete had found himself saying, "But that's really evil," and now he was thinking that, although people *could* be evil, animals really couldn't. Why was that, exactly? he wondered. Even the very fiercest predators – the ones who'd made a meal of human beings in past centuries – couldn't be called "evil." Only human beings could. And although Pete believed there *was* such a thing as evil, one of the reasons he didn't go to church any more was he'd always found himself confused by Catholic teachings when the subject came up.

Still, one of the things that had truly shocked Pete about Russell Tate and his friend Slade DeMarco was that they'd used the word in the name of their band as if they were advertising it. While you couldn't say that they'd *called* themselves that, exactly – it was more as if they were referring to the fact that evil existed, that it was part of existence – why would you want to remind yourself of that every time you picked up your musical instrument?

What *was* evil, anyway? Pete thought. He'd used the word just that morning, but he couldn't see it anywhere right now. What he saw was this really cool guy named Rafael Solares sitting at the wheel of his boat the *Rainbow Bridge,* and as Pete walked down to join him and Jupiter, he heard the tail end of a conversation they'd been having.

"Well, I don't know," Rafael was saying as he surveyed the shore near Point Conception. "I don't see any coves that would work as landing sites for a smuggling operation."

He was wearing sunglasses to shield his eyes from the glare off the water, but even so, Pete was amazed he could see the shore at all. Sitting behind the wheel with an intent expression on his face, he glanced up and down it, then shook his head again.

"You may be right that the smugglers are brash enough to dock at the marina fully loaded," he added to Jupiter. "The currents up ahead can be very strong. A hundred years ago, fourteen U.S. Navy ships were running south from San Francisco to San Diego when the lead ship mistook the light at Point Arguello for the light at Point Conception. Seven destroyers ran aground, and two of them were lost."

As he completed a sure-handed turn and pointed the *Rainbow Bridge*'s bow back toward Isla Vista, Rafael added, "The sea around here has taken a lot of men."

Pete was about to ask something about the destroyers, but just then he saw a boat with furled sails steaming along in the same direction the *Rainbow Bridge* was going. It was a boat with two masts from which cables ran to port and starboard, and it looked oddly familiar, he thought – though he really couldn't remember ever having seen a boat just like it. Then, all of a sudden, he caught a glimpse of the boat's name on the side of the hull. *Santa María,* the words read.

"Holy moly," Pete said to himself, taking a deep breath.

"What is it?" Jupiter asked him.

"Well that boat is named the *Santa María,*" he said, pointing, "and the day my mother took me to Veronica's bird shop to poke around for the first time, I saw a boat exactly like that one, with the same name on the hull, floating in one of the slips of the Rocky Beach marina. I told you and the others about it. Remember? When Rafael was visiting us in Headquarters. A Mexican guy named José was on deck."

"The same first name as the guy who Rafael bought Rojo from. I remember," Jupiter said. "Well, well, that's quite a coincidence – if that's actually what it is."

As the two of them watched the sailboat bounding over the waves, and Rafael turned his bow for home, the *Santa María* also turned, making a beeline for the marina near St. Peter's Church.

It was close to four-thirty when they arrived back at the marina in Isla Vista, and as Rafael docked his boat and the boys and Mallory helped get it moored, Jupiter looked at his watch and said they'd better hurry if they were to get to St. Peter's to check out the carillon by five. They piled into Rafael's truck, and Rafael made it to St. Peter's by 4:55. He parked and they got out, glancing at their watches and up at the steeple. At five sharp, the first note sounded. Then the second and the third. By the time the eighth note sounded, Pete leapt into the air.

"That's it!" he yelled.

"I agree," said Jupiter. "Why don't we leave the truck here and take a walk down to the water? The marina is very close."

Since Rafael knew the town, he took the lead, and Pete found himself walking next to him.

At the marina, two main piers jutted from a concrete dock that ran along the waterfront, and from each pier were floating walkways extending at ninety degrees, making slips for the sailboats and yachts and sleek racing craft harbored there. Most of the slips were occupied. Out at the far end, a man and a woman were securing their sailboat for the night.

Pete looked from boat to boat. Since the sailboat with *Santa María* painted on its hull had almost certainly docked here somewhere, all they had to do was find it. And find it they soon did. They'd been about to split up into two separate search parties when Pete saw a man emerge from the hatch of a sailboat in a nearby slip. The man was brown from the sun, had high cheekbones and a thick black mustache that covered his entire upper lip, and wore a silver chain around his neck.

"Unless there's two of him, or I'm seeing double, that's him," he said. "Back up." He pulled the others away from the dock – up behind a panel truck that was parked on the avenue that fronted the sea.

"That's José," he said. "The Mexican guy my mom and I saw at the Rocky Beach marina. When I tried to speak with him, he got real nervous. He was a nice guy, but afraid of something. Is this also *your* José?" he asked Rafael.

"I'll need to get closer and take a look. The three of you stay here and out of sight and

I'll be back shortly," Rafael said.

Pete stood with his back against the panel truck looking over his shoulder at Rafael until he realized he was imitating a guy he'd seen in a spy movie and started laughing. Even so, he and the other three kept their eyes on Rafael the whole time he was gone. He went close enough to see if he recognized the man, but stayed mostly out of sight. He hurried back to where the boys and Mallory were waiting.

"That's the guy," Rafael said. "I'd know him anywhere. So it seems that the reason he couldn't tell me where he lived was because he lived on a sailboat, making regular trips up and down the coast of California! He's really *got* to be one of the smugglers – who always work in a gang."

"I agree," said Jupiter. "The capybaras you found wandering not too far from here must have somehow gotten away from whoever it is he turns them over to when he arrives in Isla Vista with a fresh load. If Russell Tate is the brains behind the smuggling operation, and Slade DeMarco is the brawn, José must be the person bringing the animals up by boat. But whose boat, I wonder?"

"I do, too," said Rafael. "That's a very

nice ketch he just brought into the slip. It hardly seems likely to be his.”

“But who else’s could it be?” asked Pete. “Maybe I should just go over and ask him.”

The others all looked at him a bit incredulously, so he added, “No, I mean it. Really. I speak Spanish O.K., and when I met him the first time, everything was friendly.”

He thought for a moment, then added, to Rafael, “If you’d seen José yourself that day you and I met at Veronica’s, maybe he’d have pulled the plug on the whole operation. He and the *Santa María* were both there – just a hundred yards from the bird shop.”

“Which strongly suggests that I was right about Jack Cutter,” Rafael said a little grimly. “If Russell and Slade and Cutter are all part of a gang taking deliveries of illegal animals from José, then it explains José’s presence at the Rocky Beach marina and also the farmer’s market. What it *doesn’t* explain is why José was selling his pet scarlet macaw.”

“Maybe I can find out the reason he was doing that, too,” said Pete. “Whatever else we do, I don’t think *you* should approach José,” he said to Rafael. “After all, you just recently bought his scarlet macaw and asked a lot of questions. Seeing you appear totally out of the blue would certainly spook him."

"I agree," Jupiter said. "All right, then, go for it."

Pleased with the faith his friends were putting in him, Pete sauntered down to the dock, trying to seem as though he was just there to take a look at the marina. He walked out on the pier and surveyed the various yachts and sailboats, all the while getting closer to the slip where José was moored. José looked up and saw him, then hurriedly looked back down, as if he were concentrating on what he was doing.

It was now or never, Pete thought. He ventured out on the walkway closest to José. When José looked up and saw him, Pete tried to act as though he was recognizing the man for the first time.

"Hi!" he said. "¡Qué sorpresa!" What a surprise!

The expression on José's face told Pete he didn't recognize him, so in Spanish Pete reminded him that they'd met just a few days before in Rocky Beach.

"¿Recuerda?"

José looked very nervous but finally said he remembered. Pete tried to speak English, but José just shook his head in an agitated fashion. Pete thought that when he got nervous José probably had trouble with English. So Pete stuck to Spanish, keeping his sentences simple. He thought Ms. Castellano, his Spanish teacher, would have been proud — and his mother would have been even prouder.

Pete told José how beautiful his boat was. This seemed to calm the man just a little.

"Sí, sí," he said. "Amo mi velero."

Then Pete asked José what he was doing in Isla Vista. Did he live up here? The calm instantly vanished, and Pete could see the man get defensive and nervous all over again. He went back to his work, as if Pete wasn't even there. It was clear that line of inquiry wasn't going to get Pete anywhere, so he decided to simply be direct — to go for broke.

"Did you ever own a scarlet macaw named Rojo?" he asked in Spanish. "Didn't you think he was amazing?"

José was so surprised by Pete's question that he didn't have time to pretend. His hands flew up in the air, and his Spanish came out in a rush. Rojo? His uncle, who had lived in America, had died and left him two things: the sailboat and Rojo, and he loved them both very much. They were wonderful, and Rojo had been his friend. He'd kept him company when José was sailing, and he never would have parted with the bird if he hadn't been afraid that if he kept him he'd get arrested.

"Detenido?" Pete asked.

"Me encantan todos los animales," José said fervently. He loved all animals. How in the world did Pete know about Rojo?

Pete told him he was friends with the man who had bought him. José looked sad and happy at the same time, asking how the bird was. Was he well? Was he eating? He'd been afraid that, after all the years that Rojo had lived on the boat, he wouldn't take well to dry land. He was delighted to hear that the bird seemed to have adapted well.

The more José talked, the more Pete liked him. His intuition told him that José was a good man − nothing at all like Slade and not much like Pete's idea of a smuggler. In fact, Pete saw with a shock that, if things had been different and his father's parents had stayed in Mexico, his father's brothers − or even his father himself − might well have been someone like José. Martín Crenshaw had simply had more opportunities.

José was clearly happy to be reminded of Rojo, so Pete talked about the amazing noises the bird had made, and even imitated some of them — to José's vast amusement. The man applauded and applauded.

"Muy bueno!" he said.

So when Pete asked José why Rojo might have gotten him arrested, José said, without hesitation, that he'd been on deck with the bird one night in Rocky Beach, and a gringo had approached him and started talking in English.

In spite of the language difficulties, it seemed that José had been trying to be polite when all of a sudden Rojo had said something that made José feel frightened and paranoid. What if the man worked for some branch of the U.S. government? He could have lost his boat! His boat was all he had in the world, and with five children back in Mexico, he could not afford that! His boat was his livelihood.

Pete felt very sympathetic, but he couldn't resist. "Did Rojo say, 'More capybaras on the way'"? he asked.

José blanched and his hands flew up again. "Madre de Dios!" he said. "Sí, sí. Como supiste?" But then he went on — of course, Pete had met Rojo.

But why did Rojo say such an unusual thing? Pete asked, in Spanish.

A series of conflicting expressions

crossed Jose's face, as though he were wrestling with his instincts. But finally, he said he'd decided to trust Pete, because he felt so lonely, and Pete seemed like a nice boy. Although his English was very poor, he did know certain phrases. He'd been bringing these animals –

"Capybaras?" Pete asked.

Sí, sí, José said. "En Columbia, el chigüiro." He'd been bringing them up for some time now, and when he got close enough to the Isla Vista marina, he would call his partner on his cellphone and say "More capybaras on the way" so that his partner could get ready.

José didn't know how many deliveries he'd made, but Rojo had heard him say this over and over, and one day, right after José had said it, Rojo said it too. At first, José said, he had thought it was funny, and then he got frightened. How do you make a parrot unlearn something? Rojo began saying it more often, at unexpected times. After the encounter with the gringo, when José felt he couldn't risk it any more, he had taken Rojo to a market and had sold him to a nice man with a long ponytail.

"Yo comprendo," Pete said. "Lo siento."

Suddenly José frowned. "I should not

have told you any of that," he said in Spanish, "It could get me in very big trouble. You won't tell anyone, will you? Please don't tell anyone."

"No," Pete said. "Of course not."

"Prometeme," José said. Promise me.

"Yo prometo," Pete said − aware even as he said it that, although he wouldn't give José away to any authorities, he *was* going to tell Jupiter, Bob, Mallory, and Rafael everything José had said as soon as he saw them again.

"Well," Pete said in Spanish, feeling a little bit guilty, "it was nice to see you again. Adiós. Hasta la vista."

"Adiós," José said. Nervously he went back to examining a rope.

Pete started walking away, and then he started walking faster. When he got back to the others, they were more than eager to hear what he'd found out.

"We watched you the whole time," Bob said. "It looked like you did really well."

"You can say that again!" Pete said. "Wait'll you hear!"

When they did, they were all very impressed.

"So he *does* own the boat, after all," said

Rafael. "Well, I hope he can keep it. I have a feeling quite a few people would be happy to take it off his hands."

Pete hadn't really thought of that, and he felt dismayed at the thought of someone trying to steal such a nice boat from such a decent man.

"The only thing you didn't find out," Jupiter said, "was the name of the man José calls on his cellphone – the one who picks up the capybaras. I assume he's also the one who lines up buyers for them. José's partner is the missing link in the chain. But there was no way you could have found that out. If you'd asked him that, he'd have known what you were doing. You did great."

"He's such a nice guy!" Pete said. "I'm sure he doesn't think he's doing anything really wrong."

"With five children back home in Mexico," Rafael said, "he has more on his mind than American laws. Although if he's gotten involved with importing wild hyacinth macaws, he's also breaking the laws of Brazil and a bunch of other South American countries."

"All we talked about was capybaras," Pete said. "Rojo was his pet. José didn't say anything about bringing hyacinth macaws into the country."

"Yes," Jupiter said, "that's a complication we don't yet fully understand."

"Why don't we head back to my house?" Rafael said. "There's no reason to be standing around here. The sun sets at about 8:00 tonight, and you need to get your tents up. Elena works as a paralegal at a law firm in town, but by now she'll be home, and she's expecting us for dinner."

Pete was delighted to hear that. He was hungry, and soon he would be ravenous. They were walking up the hill toward the parking lot at St. Peter's when suddenly Rafael stopped short and put his arms out to either side like gates at a railroad crossing. He was staring up the street, and Pete followed his gaze to see a man who was either Jack Cutter or looked exactly like him.

"That's Jack Cutter," he said excitedly to Bob and Mallory and Jupe.

"The missing link in the chain," said Jupiter, looking toward Cutter with interest. "Which is very good news for Rafael, I think."

"What do you mean?" asked Pete.

"Well, if Jack Cutter is the guy who takes delivery of the capybaras once José has gotten them up to Isla Vista, then I don't really see what role Rafael's son Gabriel might be playing in the operation," Jupiter explained. "Before we got up here and saw what we've seen, I was thinking that maybe Gabriel had been recruited because Rafael lives in Isla Vista, and when he comes to visit his father he might provide some useful service to the gang. What useful service, I had no idea, and I also doubted that Rafael would miss something like that going on right under his nose."

"I don't know," said Rafael. "With kids, it can be hard to notice the right things and not the wrong ones."

But Pete could tell he was ready to let Jupiter persuade him that he had been wrong to be worried about what his son might be getting up to.

"The point is," Jupiter said, "if Jack Cutter is moving back and forth between Rocky Beach and Isla Vista, then there really would be no need to introduce a fifth member into the gang. And even though both Russell and Slade strike me as pretty reckless, I doubt they would want a person as young as Gabriel working with them, anyway," he added.

That made sense to Pete – and to Rafael, too. In fact, he looked as if what Jupiter had just said had lightened an invisible burden he'd been carrying ever since Pete had first seen him. He looked almost jaunty. "Well, who's going to follow young Cutter back to his lair, then?" he asked. "Not me. I'm far too recognizable. Can you guys follow him and see what he's up to?"

He looked at the four of them who were all nodding vigorously.

"Call me on my cellphone as soon as you have any information, or if you need any help," Rafael added. "I'll be waiting to hear from you, and to come pick you up. O.K.?"

"You bet!" Pete said. "We'll find out where he's going!"

Rafael smiled and nodded, then swiftly walked away. To the west, the sun was starting its long descent toward the horizon, and it seemed to Pete as though Rafael had vanished in a blaze of golden light. He hadn't, of course. He'd just turned the corner.

But although the man was, in most ways, entirely normal, Pete still liked him more and more the longer he was around him. Part of what he liked about him was how natural he had been with The Three Investigators ever since he'd met them, but part of it was also how much he seemed to care about his son. If you cared about animals and teenagers − not

to mention caring about making sure that teenagers were taught how to be around animals —
then you had a lot going for you, Pete thought.

Anyway, it was great that they'd bumped
into Jack Cutter, and that they were about to
start trailing him to wherever he was heading
next!

10

An Electrifying Phone Call

As Jupiter saw Rafael disappear around the corner, he wasn't quite as happy as Pete was with the current situation. It had been a pretty long day already, and Jupiter hadn't expected to spend the next who-knew-how-long trailing a suspected bad guy. In fact, he'd been looking forward to getting back to Rafael and Elena's house, having a meal, putting up the tents, then talking around a fire.

Of course, he, Pete, and Bob had trailed people before, but they'd never done it on the streets of an unfamiliar town, and Jupiter thought he'd better take charge of their reconnaissance mission before Jack Cutter also disappeared.

"Now, this is obvious," he told the others, "but I'll say it, anyway. It's O.K. if Jack Cutter sees us, but we can't let him figure out that we're following him. So whatever you do, don't look at him too often or watch him too closely. Pay a lot of attention to one another. Act as naturally as you can."

"Maybe we should break up into groups

of two," Pete said.

"I don't think so," Jupiter said. "Jack Cutter won't ever suspect he's being followed by four people. Our very visibility will make us invisible."

Jupiter saw that Pete was champing at the bit, so before he could do anything rash, Jupiter said, "Let's go!" and the four of them took off after their quarry – who seemed to be in no particular hurry. He was sauntering along with earbuds in his ears, clicking his fingers to the tempo of the music, and kicking small pebbles on the sidewalk. Nevertheless, he hardly seemed relaxed. He was carrying a smartphone in his hand, and although at the moment it was playing music, from time to time he glanced at it as if he were waiting for it to ring.

"Slow down!" Pete hissed. "We don't want to get too close!"

Despite Pete's admonition, they kept gaining on Cutter, and when Jupiter thought they were too close, he led the way across the street so that they were almost opposite their target. For the first time, Jupiter got a good look at him.

He looked much as Rafael had described him the day he'd come to the Salvage Yard.

His hair was whitish-blond, very fine, and shoulder-length, gathered into a ponytail with a rubber band. Under his lower lip sprouted a tuft of hair that Jupiter thought made him look silly.

Jack Cutter was young – in his late 20s, Jupiter thought – and he was wearing a dark t-shirt with ANIMAL LOVER in big white block letters printed on the front, a pair of blue jeans with holes in both knees, and a pair of sandals. The expression on his face kept shifting from relaxation to anxiety and back again. They were now several blocks from the water-front, and as he approached the corner of a block, Cutter took the earbuds out of his ears, slowed down, and ducked under a green-striped awning into a small bodega.

"Come on," Jupiter said, and the others followed him back across the street and into the store. At the front, behind a counter with a register, a woman with heart-shaped glasses smiled at them as they walked in. For a moment, Jupiter couldn't find their quarry, but then he saw him at a wall cooler, examining the pre-made sandwiches. Bob and Mallory pretended to argue about whether to get pretzels or potato chips.

"That's great," Jupiter whispered. "But I

think we should actually buy something or it might look suspicious."

Bob grabbed, almost at random, a bag of cheese curls, a small package of unshelled pistachios, and some potato chips. Each of them also took a bottle of orange juice from a cooler. Pete said, "Dinner?" and then, before anyone could answer, grabbed six sandwiches from the wall cooler Cutter had just vacated. Although Jupiter knew it was almost dinner time – and that Elena's dinner had just been postponed – he really wasn't all that hungry. Pete's stomach was a marvel, he thought.

Jack Cutter was already at the counter with his sandwich and a soda. As he paid the woman and made for the door, Jupiter thought fast.

"Just put what you've got on the counter," he said to Pete and Mallory. "Bob can stay behind and pay, while the rest of us can keep following."

Outside, Jupiter thought for a moment they'd managed to lose their man before he saw that Cutter had made a left and was heading toward a small park just up the block. You couldn't even really call it a park, Jupiter thought – just a few picnic tables and benches and some trees stunted by the salty air and offshore winds. Cutter settled at a picnic table, popped the top on his soda, then put his cellphone in front of him.

For the moment, Jupiter, Pete, and Mallory pretended to be interested in a poster stapled to a pole, but when Bob finally joined them holding a paper bag, the four of them took seats at a picnic table not far from where Cutter was unwrapping his sandwich.

Jupiter had to admit he didn't really know what he expected to happen next. Cutter seemed nervous and jumpy, but he certainly didn't look as though he had a destination – or if he did, he was in no hurry to get there. Nonetheless, Jupiter thought that Rafael had been right to think he should be followed. The very fact that he was here in Isla Vista was either a truly amazing coincidence or hard evidence that he and José were connected.

When Jupiter noticed that Bob and Pete kept looking over at Cutter, he told them to relax and talk and laugh – and also eat. Pete didn't have to be urged twice. He ripped open the bag of cheese curls and started devouring them – which turned out to be just the ticket, as far as Jupiter was concerned. Soon, Bob and Mallory were making jokes about Pete's appetite and Pete was looking up at them and smiling, wiping orange dust from around his mouth. Bob pulled out the map he'd brought with him from Rocky Beach and unfolded it in front of them.

The four of them sipped orange juice and pretended to study the map, while Cutter ate his sandwich. Mallory opened the bag of pistachios and carefully shelled twenty or thirty of them, then set them on the bag. Jupiter ate some, then began actually studying the map. He saw the marina where José was keeping his sailboat; he saw Point Conception; and he saw the Channel Islands – a series of eight islands that stretched along the coast from Santa Barbara down to Los Angeles.

The closest – Santa Cruz Island – was about twenty-five miles offshore and part of Channel Islands National Park. The furthest were Santa Catalina and San Clemente. Jupiter knew that the former was inhabited, and that the latter was operated by the United States Navy. As Jupiter and the others continued to look at the map, Jack Cutter's phone began to ring. Jupiter glanced over in time to see Cutter check the screen to see who was calling, look both irritated and relieved, then click the phone to accept the call.

"Russell?" he said, his voice a bit edged.

"Hey, man, I've been waiting. Where are you, anyway?"

Jupiter was electrified. He saw that Pete, Bob, and Mallory were all staring avidly at Cutter and nodded for them to look away. They started staring at the map as though their lives depended on it.

"Yeah, yeah," Cutter said. "All I know is that you and Slade were supposed to be here hours ago. We got a *schedule*, man. José's boat is in the slip, and we're supposed to be delivering two of the big packages tomorrow – down the coast by Rocky Beach." He stopped and listened for a minute. "Well, how are we supposed to get them from the warehouse to the boat? All I've got is my Indian, and José can't sail his boat up to the warehouse. We need your panel truck."

Jupiter could hear every word Cutter was saying. He was making no attempt to talk softly or to watch what he said.

"What? You're kidding me," he said. "I've got buyers for all eight of them. Papers, too. The four you had were stolen? Why didn't Slade just leave them here with the others? They would have been totally safe."

Cutter continued to talk as though he were alone in the world, and, not for the first time, Jupiter marveled at how cellphones had changed the rules of human interaction. Wherever they were – at the dinner table, on a busy street, in line at the supermarket, in a doctor's waiting room – most people using cellphones acted as though no one could hear them – as though the phones created a private bubble in which the conversation took place.

In old movies Jupiter had frequently seen people in phone booths who carefully closed the door between the phone and the rest of the world, so that they could speak in private. But cellphones had removed the very idea of privacy. People no longer seemed to have any understanding of how many people could overhear them, or how far their voices carried.

Normally, Jupiter thought this behavior was both foolish and inconsiderate, but right now he was thrilled that Jack Cutter didn't seem to care who heard his conversation. Cellphones were an eavesdropper's dream.

"You don't have to tell *me* Slade's paranoid," Cutter said. "But those bir... small packages were your cut of the last import, and the four in the warehouse are ours." He paused. "No, I won't. José may be scared of you, but I'm getting tired of this. Even when you were only taking 30%, I didn't like being blackmailed, and I'm not going to give up $40,000 in bir... small packages just because your muscle man is a loser."

Jack Cutter really didn't like Slade, Jupiter thought.

"He probably takes steroids," Cutter said. "Yes, that's what I said. He's a muscle man muscle man and a loser loser. Heh heh heh. Oh, really? What are you going to do to me? For package imports like these, it's just little fines. If José hadn't been scared his boat would be seized, we'd never have gone along with any of this to begin with."

After this long exchange, Cutter fell silent for a while. Jupiter glanced at the others, who still stared at the map but clearly weren't seeing anything. With the sun continuing its slow progress toward the horizon, the temperature was dropping as the water off the ocean cooled the shore. From across the city, Jupiter could hear the wail of a siren.

At the next table, Cutter was listening carefully to whatever Russell Tate was saying, and Jupiter could only imagine that Russell had started playing Mr. Nice Guy after his attempt at intimidation had failed.

"Yeah," Cutter said. "O.K. I get you. Let's just deal with the four big packages for

Rocky Beach delivery now. We can worry about the small ones later. O.K. I'll be waiting. See you soon."

He got up from the bench where he'd been sitting, stretched, and slipped his phone into his pocket. Then he gathered the trash left from his dinner and was on his way to a trash can when a young woman came into the park with two dogs on leashes. One was long and brown and white, with a happy and comical face, a little overweight, with two flaring perky ears. Jupiter might have been mistaken – he was certainly no dog expert – but he thought it was called a corgi. The other was much smaller – a Chihuahua or something – and as soon as he saw them, Cutter dumped his trash and went over to the woman.

He asked politely if it was O.K. if he said hello to the dogs, and although the woman looked a little suspicious – as if she thought he might be more interested in her than he was in her dogs – she said yes. Instantly Cutter was on his knees in the dirt, letting the dogs sniff the back of his hand, and – when they'd accepted him – rubbing their heads and behind their ears. All the time he did this he was also cooing – saying how good they were, how handsome they were, how nice they were and so on.

He seemed very familiar with dogs, and certainly looked as if he loved them. When he got back to his feet, he told the woman how great her corgi was – Jupiter was pleased to hear he'd been right – and that he'd always wanted one. He said he worked in a bird shop and that he liked birds a lot, but that he had three dogs himself. He loved dogs.

The woman pointed to Cutter's t-shirt and said that it looked like that was true. And when Cutter looked down at his chest, where he'd advertised that he was an ANIMAL LOVER, he started laughing.

Suddenly Jupiter liked him. He'd seemed a little rough on the phone with Russell, and maybe he'd been trying to act tougher than he was. He certainly didn't give off an air of menace the way both Slade DeMarco and Russell Tate had when Jupiter met them. Jupiter had to concede that Cutter might well be a nice guy. He seemed utterly sincere about his love of animals. As Jupiter watched, he hunkered down and started fooling around with the dogs again.

"Such a good girl," he said to the Chihuahua. "You're so pretty."

Jupiter got to his feet and nodded to the

others, suggesting with gestures that they leave the park while Cutter was still talking with the woman. They deposited their trash in a green wire basket, then reconvened down the block in front of a clothing store – pretending to window shop.

"That phone call was perfect," Bob said. "It confirmed everything we've guessed, and then some."

"It really did," Mallory said. "But what was that about the Indian?"

"I think he meant an Indian motorbike," said Pete.

Jupiter agreed with Pete's interpretation, but he was eager to get on to what they'd just learned. He looked at the other three and they all signaled that they were listening, so he proceeded.

"It sounds as though José and Jack Cutter had a small operation in place, importing animals from South America – mainly capybaras, I presume. Maybe *only* capybaras. Somehow Russell Tate or Slade DeMarco found out about it and started to lean on them."

He paused to gather his thoughts, and while he did, Bob said, "Maybe Russell was curious about where the capybaras Rafael had given Wally had come from and started to ask around about it. Maybe he found someone else with capybaras, asked where he'd gotten them, and got Jack Cutter's name."

"Great thinking, Records," Jupiter said. "I bet that's exactly how it happened. Russell knew his father's animals were illegal, and he thought maybe he could get in on the action somehow. It seems to have begun as simple blackmail — with the threat of José and Jack Cutter being exposed to the authorities — but it's turned into something larger now."

"Yes," Mallory said. "Cutter said, 'even when you only were taking thirty percent,' — which implies that their demands have grown. Maybe the capybaras didn't produce a high enough profit, so Russell pressured José to start bringing in animals with a larger price tag."

"Maybe José met Jack Cutter through his uncle," Pete said, "and when the uncle died and left José the boat and Rojo, they cooked up the original plan. If José really has five children, he probably needs all the money he can get."

"That sounds plausible," Jupiter said.

"Yes," Bob agreed. "Jack Cutter found buyers for the capybaras, while José brought them up on his boat. Although it was illegal, no one was getting hurt — especially the capybaras." He turned to Mallory and said, "We learned that capybaras can live to be twelve years old in captivity, and in the wild they're lucky if a jaguar doesn't get them by the time they're four."

"Cutter's good with animals," Pete said. "At least he sure likes dogs, and he was wearing that t-shirt. José too, I think. He told me he loves all animals, and I believed him. So those two guys were probably taking good care of any animals they imported. That's a plus."

"Yes," Jupiter said. "As Bob said, no one was getting hurt. At least, not until Russell and Slade barged in. They're clearly in it only for the money; they don't care about animals at all. Not only that, but now Slade and Russell are demanding fifty percent – they seem to have claimed they were entitled to four of the eight hyacinth macaws José brought up on his boat."

"And after we rescued the four Slade took back to Rocky Beach, it sounded like Russell was demanding two of the four that were left," Bob said.

As Bob finished this sentence, Jupiter noticed that Cutter was on his feet again. He waved goodbye to the woman with the dogs and started to move quite quickly, as though he'd lingered in the park longer than he'd realized and now had to make up for lost time.

Jupiter watched him walk to the corner across the street from where they were looking in the window, then turn right. Pretending to laugh and talk, Jupiter and the others followed him another four blocks to a small industrial building of corrugated iron, measuring about twenty-four feet square.

It looked more like a machine shed than a warehouse, but it was big enough for some capybaras and some hyacinth macaws. When Cutter got there, he turned into the parking lot and walked past an Indian motorbike – old and beat up, but clearly well-loved – which he patted as he passed.

Taking a key from his pocket, he let himself into the warehouse. Jupiter wanted to go in himself, but it was impossible right now. He motioned to the others to withdraw, so they retreated across the street. The sun was still sinking toward the horizon, but it wasn't even close to setting, and they were all extremely visible.

It was time to call Rafael, Jupiter decided. Bob got out his cellphone and dialed the number, and although it seemed a long time before Rafael arrived in his truck, it actually took only ten minutes. Jupiter explained what had happened.

"Slade and Russell will probably be getting here any time now, and from the sounds of Jack Cutter's conversation, they're going to show up in a panel truck," Jupiter said. "When they get here, I think they're going to be taking four capybaras down to José's boat." He paused and pinched his lip.

"Some people might think we should call the authorities right about now," Rafael said, "but since all of you think José and Cutter are decent guys being muscled by Slade and Russell, I'm not eager to turn them in."

"Me, neither!" Pete said emphatically. "I think two of us should stake out José's boat, and the rest of us should stay here. That way, we'll be able to see what really goes down."

"That sounds like a plan," Rafael said. "I'll drive Pete and Bob back to the marina. They can be on stake-out duty. If José sees them for some reason, at least he already knows Pete, and I don't think he'll find you threatening, Bob. Then the rest of us can come back here. If Russell shows up, I'll try to talk some sense into him. I've known him for thirty years and I may be able to make a dent. On the other hand, he knows how much I dislike him, so I'm probably not the best messenger."

Pete, Bob, and Mallory crawled in the back of Rafael's pickup, while Jupiter climbed in front. Soon Rafael was parking the truck in the lot at St. Peter's again, and they all piled out.

Jupiter cautioned Pete and Bob. "Watch José's boat but stay out of sight," he said. "And take two of the walkie-talkies. We've got the other two. Bob, you have your cellphone, right?"

Bob said he did, and although Jupiter knew that Rafael also had one, he was chagrined that neither he nor Pete had brought theirs.

"Anyway," he said, "if we're going to be separated, the walkie-talkies will keep us in touch. They're good for over thirty miles."

"That should work," Bob said, "since we'll only be a couple of blocks from each other."

"If Bob and I are going to wait down here, at least we should eat," Pete said. "Who has the bag with the sandwiches?"

Bob was still their custodian, and he gave three of them to Jupiter and Mallory and kept three of them for him and Pete.

Bob and Pete grabbed their backpacks

and Jupiter rooted around in an equipment bag and found the walkie-talkies. He handed them out, and he, Pete, Bob, and Mallory all turned them on and made sure they were on the same channel. Jupiter also grabbed a flashlight. It might come in handy.

"O.K.," Pete said. "See you guys later." He turned to walk down toward the water, then paused and waited for Bob. When the two of them got out onto the street, they turned and waved to Jupiter, Mallory, and Rafael, and for a moment, Jupiter had an uneasy feeling watching them walk away.

11

Mallory Crosses A Threshold

Mallory watched Pete and Bob walk down toward the marina, but as they vanished around a corner, she turned toward the parking lot at St. Peter's, leading the way to Rafael's yellow truck. She and Jupiter were both mostly silent on the short drive back to the warehouse; once again, Mallory sat by the door with the window open, wondering what would happen next.

She was still really pleased that her insight about the carillon had led The Three Investigators to St. Peter's-by-the-Sea and the boat on which Rojo had once lived, and that she had been asked to come on this adventure. But she also thought it would have been nice to be getting ready for dinner at Rafael's house right now and putting up tents in his backyard – to have been relaxing with Jupiter, Pete, and Bob.

This was especially true because Mallory had an aversion to ugly buildings, and the warehouse to which they were driving was a hideous square made of rusting corrugated panels. When they reached it, Rafael drove slowly past as Mallory and Jupiter stared. It stood on a lot that looked abandoned, with its weeds and tall grass, its accumulation of junk. In one corner was an old dumpster, its lid flung back – but as they drove past, Mallory noticed that Jack Cutter's Indian motorbike was missing.

"Look," said Mallory. "The motorbike's gone."

"So it is," Jupiter said, peering past her from the middle of the seat. "That means that Jack Cutter is also gone."

Rafael drove around the block and parked at a corner from which he could keep an eye on the warehouse's door. He shut off the engine.

"Maybe their plans have changed," he said. "Maybe the rendezvous was postponed until after dark. If I were trying to smuggle capybaras around Isla Vista, I'd think of using darkness as a cover."

"Maybe," Jupiter said. "Capybaras can get really big, but it seems only logical that José and Jack Cutter have been selling juvenile animals – ones that weigh no more than thirty or forty pounds. If so, they could be carried in plastic kennels with wire doors – maybe even the kind with plastic handles on the top. You wouldn't need darkness to carry animals around in kennels like that."

"That's true," said Rafael. "My logical faculties keep failing me. Some of those kennels even have wheels on the bottom. Although José's boat is a lot bigger than mine is, even big old ketches can have small cabins, so it makes sense they'd be smuggling juvenile animals. We'd know if we could get inside that warehouse."

"We ought to do that," Mallory said. "We think the warehouse is being used to keep animals in, but we have no real evidence."

"I agree," Jupiter said. "Why don't you wait with the truck, Rafael, while Mallory and I see what we can do? We have a lot more latitude than you have, as an adult. If neighbors see us poking around, they won't think anything about it."

"All right," Rafael said. "But keep your ears open. If anyone shows up, I'll hit the horn twice."

Rafael seemed pretty relaxed, under the circumstances, but Mallory was suddenly feeling a bit tense. Like Jupiter, she tended to think ahead – to anticipate contingencies – and one of the contingencies she suddenly anticipated was getting caught inside the warehouse when Russell and Slade showed up. Although she'd never met them, they sounded nasty, and possibly dangerous, and even if Rafael was nearby, with his truck, that wouldn't help if Mallory and Jupiter were cornered inside. Still, they were committed to the exploration now.

They strolled through the weedy and disheveled area around the warehouse as though they belonged there. Trying to make himself look casual, Jupiter tested the handle on the door. It was locked, so they continued around to the back. Since the front and sides presented an impenetrable façade, Mallory was surprised to find three small rectangular windows.

"Look at that," Jupiter said. "This one isn't locked. In fact, it's open a crack. That's good. It means if we get inside the building, we won't have committed any crime."

"We won't?" Mallory asked.

"No," Jupiter said. "For breaking and entering, there has to be breaking, and just entering somewhere is legal unless there's a sign saying that it's not. There's no sign here. We just need something to stand on."

He looked around, saw an old wooden vegetable crate, put it under the window, and stood on it. Once he was up, he was able to open the window wide. Standing on tiptoe next to him, all Mallory could see was a metal interior wall.

"Do you want to climb in?" she asked.

As if in response, there was a sharp shriek, followed by some whistling and grunting.

"Macaws and capybaras, I presume," Jupiter said, mildly. "I'll go first, and you can follow."

Mallory watched as he pushed himself up, stuck his torso inside the window, then wiggled forward enough so that he could wrestle his legs around and get them underneath him. At one point, his pants got caught on a nail, and − halfway in and hallway out of the building − he worked the cloth free of the metal, then dropped to the floor. He took the flashlight from his pocket and turned it on.

Mallory followed, and when she was inside, the grunting got louder. Together, she and Jupiter made their way down a metal-walled corridor until they reached a door into the main part of the building.

There, in the flashlight's halo, Mallory saw six young capybaras in two large pens looking up expectantly. Jupiter had been right in guessing they'd be juveniles and that they would fit quite nicely into plastic kennels, of which there were six lined up by the wall.

"They must be transporting the capybaras to and from the boat in those carriers," she said. "You were right. I'm glad to see that when they're here, they're kept in a pen together."

Next to the capybaras' pens was another empty pen, and as Mallory looked around her, she saw that Jack Cutter had actually been taking care of the animals very well. The pens contained hay, large bowls of water, and some cereal-looking stuff Mallory assumed was capybara food, while to the side of the pens was an empty plastic wading pool next to a drain in the floor.

A hose snaked across the concrete and into the empty pool, and since the concrete was still wet, Mallory assumed the capybaras had had a bath or a swim quite recently. She remembered that they were semi-aquatic, and although a plastic pool was no substitute for a river or a swamp, still it was something.

Hearing a loud, insistent squawk, she looked up and saw four blue birds in large cages. The hyacinth macaws. They were really very beautiful – and somehow both sturdy and fragile at one and the same time. Up until now, she hadn't really focused on how wrong it was to take these lovely creatures so far from their jungle homes, but now that she saw them, she no longer wished she was at Rafael and Elena's house; she was glad she was here with Jupiter, getting information that could put a stop to this particular branch of the illegal animal trade.

There was another bird there, too – a bird with an eye rimmed with yellow, and a brilliant red head.

"That's Rojo," Jupiter said.

When he heard his name, Rojo let out a shriek. He, too, was very beautiful, Mallory thought – but a second thought followed swiftly on the first. Rojo had only been stolen from Three Investigators Headquarters two days before, and that meant he'd been brought here very recently. What if *very recently* meant today? This evening, even?

After all, as she studied the macaws, Mallory noticed that their food bowls – clipped to the sides of the cages – were filled to the brim with seeds and nuts. Their water bottles were also full, and new paper had been put on the cages' floors. And then she remembered the empty pen next to the capybaras.

"Oh, no!" she said. "I just realized that the only way Rojo would even *be* here would be if Slade DeMarco or Russell Tate brought him. What if they've already been and gone? When Cutter was talking to Russell, I got the impression they hadn't talked for a while."

Jupiter looked startled at this insight, then nodded and gestured to the empty pen next to the capybaras.

"The birds and capybaras have all been fed and watered and taken care of, so Cutter may be gone for the night and not coming back," he said. "I can't believe it didn't occur to me earlier that Russell and Slade could have also already come and gone. If so, they're on their way to José's boat. Which means – "

"They could easily run into Pete and Bob," Mallory said. "Maybe we should go. Should we take Rojo with us? I hate to leave him here."

Mallory lifted Rojo's cage off its hook, and soon the two of them were back at the window. Outside, the wooden crate was still in place, so Mallory handed Rojo's cage to Jupiter, climbed up on a wooden chair, then clambered down onto the crate. Jupiter handed Rojo out, then followed Mallory. By now, the sun which had been gradually sinking toward the horizon was almost down, and in a little while it would be starting to get dark, Mallory thought.

Almost running, she and Jupiter took off for Rafael's truck; when they got there, they explained the situation and put Rojo in the back. On the way to the marina, Jupiter tried to get Bob and Pete on the walkie-talkie.

He turned it on and pushed the TALK button. "Second? Records? Are you there? Come in, please. Over."

The device screeched, but there was no response.

Determined, Jupiter punched the TALK button again. "Pete?" he said. "Bob? Come in, please. Over."

Still no response. "They don't seem to be hearing me," he said. "The range is certainly short enough. I'll try again when we get closer to the marina."

Mallory could see that Jupiter was trying to seem calm, but he was obviously very worried, and when they got to the marina, he no longer tried to hide it. Mallory knew his worst fears had been confirmed. José was gone, the boat was gone, and Bob and Pete were nowhere to be seen.

As Mallory watched, Jupiter tried the walkie-talkie again, his voice increasingly anxious and rising in both tone and volume.

When again there was no answer, he asked Rafael to try Bob's cellphone, and Mallory stood there as he punched Bob's number and held the phone to his ear. Rafael shook his head, grimacing as the phone rang and rang and then went to voicemail.

"I hate to say this," Jupiter said, "because I don't like to jump to dire conclusions. But I fear that Pete and Bob have been abducted by Russell and Slade."

"I hate to say I agree with you," Rafael said. "That does seem the most likely scenario."

"Maybe we should call the police," Mallory said, "or the Coast Guard. One of them ought to be able to intercept José's boat."

"That would normally be a sound idea," Jupiter said, "but the truth is, we're only guessing. We don't know where Pete and Bob are. They could have walked into Isla Vista to get something more to eat, and their walkie-talkies could have accidentally gotten set to a different channel. Maybe Slade and Russell never showed up here. Maybe Pete and Bob got on the boat with José of their own free will. That last is highly unlikely, but since it's possible, I think contacting the police at this point would be a mistake."

As Rafael, Jupiter, and Mallory stood on the pier, looking at what Mallory would have sworn was an empty ocean, Rafael pulled a pair of binoculars from his pocket and peered through them. "You won't believe this, but I think I can see the *Santa María*. If so, we'll save a lot of time if we just go after it ourselves."

"But your boat's not even here!" Mallory said. "It's at the other marina."

"True enough," Rafael said, "but I know these waters. As soon as we get out on the ocean, we'll make good time. Even though it'll be dark soon, I've often been at sea at night."

The three of them seemed to make up their minds at the same moment, and without another word, they ran back to Rafael's truck. As he drove toward the second marina, he pulled out his cellphone to call Elena – but when he saw the screen, he said, "Wally Tate tried to reach me earlier – not long after we parted from Pete and Bob. I wonder what he wanted."

He called Elena to tell her what had happened, then put his phone away. They rode in silence until Jupiter spoke.

"I'm sorry to say this isn't the first time this summer I've had to chase Pete," he said.

Mallory knew what he meant. Pete had

briefly been held hostage by the counterfeiter André Laurent.

"He seems to have a knack for trouble," she said as lightly as she could.

Actually, she didn't feel light about it at all; somehow both she and Jupiter had failed to see that, in the time between when Rafael's truck had arrived to pick them up and the time she and Jupiter had returned to the warehouse, Slade and Russell might have eluded them, and she didn't like to think of Pete and Bob having to deal with them – much less having to deal with them alone.

"Or trouble has a knack for Pete," Jupiter said. "It's lucky he's so brave and bears up well under difficult circumstances."

Three minutes later, Rafael had come to a stop in the parking lot by the second marina.

"Grab your backpacks," he said as he threw open the back of the truck and took Rojo's cage. "You'll need them. As for this scarlet fellow, we can't leave him in the truck overnight."

They hurried up the pier to the slip where Rafael's boat was moored. They dropped their backpacks and Mallory's sleeping bag into the bow, then climbed in after their gear as Rafael hurried to the wheelhouse carrying Rojo's cage. Jupiter and Mallory followed, finding places to sit behind him as he turned on the engines and took off after the *Santa María*.

"How do you know which way they went after you saw them?" Mallory asked.

"I can't know for sure," Rafael said, "but I have to assume they're headed south. You heard Jack Cutter say they were supposed to deliver the capybaras somewhere close to Rocky Beach tomorrow. If we haven't found them by morning − or if you can't make contact with Pete and Bob − we'll call the Coast Guard and ask for help."

Mallory was relieved to hear that − so relieved that she suddenly felt hungry and thirsty and a little tired. Up until now, the adrenaline that had shot through her when she realized that Pete and Bob might be in trouble had kept her jittery, but now that there was nothing more to do but just keep going, she could think of things like food again.

"Would you like a sandwich?" she asked Rafael. "We have three of them."

"I'd love a sandwich," Rafael said. "And I've got six or seven gallons of water in milk cartons. Just grab one and pour it out." He pointed to a shallow cupboard. "You should also find a bunch of power bars."

Against the rush of wind sweeping over the bow, Mallory walked to where she'd left her backpack, pulled out the three sandwiches she'd gotten from Bob, and returned to the back of the boat. There she got the water and power bars, then handed the food and water around. She noticed that Rafael was going fairly slowly just now, and when she asked, he said that since he hadn't seen the *Santa María* again since that first sighting, he wanted to make sure he didn't pass the boat on the sea.

As long as it was still light out, he would keep this pace up, he said – and after it was dark, he would go, if anything, even slower.

Neither Jupiter nor Rafael seemed interested in talking – and Mallory wasn't either, at the moment. After a while she made her way back to the bow. As the sun dropped below the horizon, it started to get dark, but the food and water had revived her, and as Mallory looked at the sea and sky, it seemed the colors were all variants on the colors of the hyacinth macaws.

Mallory had always imagined that night on the sea would seem black, but in this strange twilight period, it seemed blue. Blue and magical, she thought – although she usually didn't like that word much. She really wasn't chilly, but something about the growing darkness and the ocean's waves on the hull suggested to her that she unstrap her sleeping bag from her backpack and stuff it behind her as she sat with her back against the bow, and her legs stretched out in front of her.

From where she was sitting, she couldn't see Rafael at the wheel, but she saw Jupiter sitting near him, and although she was a much shyer – or more private – person than he was, she really liked being on the boat with him. She also had an intuition that her role in the current case was over and done with now. Or maybe she just suddenly felt that she didn't really have to be either useful or clever at the moment. All she needed was to be there, with Jupiter Jones, on a boat on the Pacific Ocean.

It was funny, she thought, but this week she seemed to have crossed a lot of thresholds – both literal and metaphoric. Her unexpected entrance into Headquarters had been the first one, and another one had come along when she and Jupiter had climbed though the window of the warehouse. The moment Jupiter had gotten stuck on a nail, halfway in and halfway out, could stand for a less literal moment in her own life, Mallory thought.

Indeed, as the *Rainbow Bridge* motored south, occasionally coming down hard on the far side of waves, Mallory thought that, for a while now – ever since her father had died so suddenly – she, too, had been halfway in and halfway out a window. Not stuck on a nail, exactly, but still not able to move either backwards or forwards. Now she was speeding into the future – sometimes backwards, sometimes forwards, but always putting the past behind her.

Not completely, of course – she still loved and missed her father – but enough so that she could be glad to be alive again. As she sat nestled against her sleeping bag, smelling the intoxicating air, she also thought it was a great relief to sometimes let the reins drop – to let other people make decisions about where to go and what to do next. To accept that you couldn't always be in charge of your own destiny or anyone else's. To go along for the ride.

When she'd been bothered by the thought that she wouldn't be spending the evening at Rafael's house with the boys, Mallory had had no way of seeing what really lay ahead, but now she was glad that things had turned out as they had. Of course, she wasn't glad that Bob and Pete had been kidnapped, and might be frightened — or in worse trouble than she liked to think about — but she was glad that she and Jupiter were going after them on such a lovely night.

In fact, maybe moving back to Rocky Beach from Scotland after her father died had been a stroke of luck on a magnitude she didn't fully comprehend yet. Mallory clambered into her sleeping bag, then lay with her hands behind her head, looking at Jupiter's silhouette as he gazed at the waves breaking across the bow.

12

Bob And Pete Go Missing

Hours earlier, as Bob and Pete had walked down the hill from St. Peter's-by-the-Sea, Bob had felt a chill as they approached the waterfront. Now that the sun was getting lower, it was getting cooler, but what Bob was feeling had less to do with the temperature and more with the fact that he missed the solidarity he'd felt when he, Pete, Jupiter, and Mallory had all been together.

Besides, Bob liked to know what his task was at any given moment, and he wasn't sure he understood what he and Pete were supposed to be doing. All Jupiter had said was that they should stake out José's boat. Was he supposed to make regular reports to Jupiter, while Jupiter made regular reports to him and Pete about what was happening back at the warehouse? If so, Jupiter had been silent so far.

Bob took off his backpack, found the light jacket he'd brought, and put it on. There was a stretch of narrow sand in front of them, and to the right, a couple of hundred yards away, the two piers of the marina jutted out into the blue-green water. There were still boats coming in and out, and a festive air about the bustle at the piers.

Bob sensed that Pete was feeling good, and sure enough, his friend was almost giddy with the pleasure of the unexpected.

"Isn't this great?" Pete said. "I mean, you and Jupe can sit around all day, coming up with theories and leaving me in the dust – ."

"We don't do that," Bob said.

"Well," Pete said, "maybe not, but the two of you are better at it than I am. But I'm pretty good at this other stuff – tracking suspects, talking to Mexicans, staking out boats."

"You're great at it," Bob said.

"Are you hungry?" Pete asked. "Because I'm starving." He pointed to the bag Bob was carrying and motioned toward the beach. The city had built an asphalt path on the edge of the sand – between the beach and the street that ran along it. Bob supposed it was used for running and biking, or just strolling, but at intervals the city had also placed benches for the more sedentary types who wanted to sit and stare at the ocean. They were pretty basic, but they gave the boys somewhere to perch while Pete's stomach hijacked the action.

Bob thought there were many wonders

in the universe, but one of them was certainly Pete Crenshaw's metabolism. He didn't seem to have a smidgen of fat on him. He was lean and taut and muscled and always hungry. No matter how much he ate, he never gained an ounce.

Eagerly, Pete reached into the bag that Bob had been carrying and pulled out three cellophane-wrapped sandwiches. He handed one to Bob, then opened the other and began eating. Bob thought he might as well keep his stamina up, so he ripped the cellophane and examined the sandwich. To his surprise, it was fresh and delicious − lettuce, tomato, cheese, and turkey on rye bread. He was hungrier than he'd known, and when Pete offered him half of the third sandwich, he gratefully accepted.

As they ate, they watched the waves roll in. Pete finished his half of the second sandwich, then peeked in the bag to see if there was anything left. There wasn't, so he rolled the top of the bag closed and stood up.

"Time to go," he said. "We need to see what's up."

Bob smiled. Pete was really loving this − and suddenly Bob was, too. He followed as Pete walked down the path in the direction of the marina, pausing when he came to a tall green trash barrel into which he put the paper bag. At that moment, Bob's cellphone rang. He had taken it out of his backpack and put it in his pocket, and now he pulled it out, flipped it open, and saw that Walter Tate was calling.

"Hello?" he said. "This is Bob Andrews."

"I'm glad to reach you," Wally said. "I just tried to call Rafael, but my call went straight to voice mail. Is Rafael with you?" he added.

"No," Bob answered. "We've split into two groups. He and Jupe and Mallory are together, and Pete and I are by ourselves. If you want to speak to Rafael, I can call Jupe on my walkie-talkie."

"That's all right," said Wally. "But when you see him again, please tell him I've just discovered that Russell has been stealing from me. Though I hate to be so blunt about it. I gave him a Power of Attorney about a year ago, and my bank just called to ask me about some mysterious withdrawals. Russell seems to have taken a home equity loan out on my house, and since I know that Rafael's girlfriend is a paralegal, I was hoping she could sort this out."

"I'm really sorry, Mr. Tate," Bob said.

"I mean Wally. I'll be sure to give Rafael the message when I see him again."

"Many thanks," Wally said.

"Goodbye," Bob said. He slipped his phone back into his pocket, then glanced at his watch. It had been about an hour and a half since they'd followed Cutter to the warehouse and called Rafael, and about a half hour since they'd split from the others.

Bob had the impulse to raise Jupiter on the walkie-talkie but then thought better of it. What if he and Mallory and Rafael were all involved in some scene with Russell Tate? Better to let Jupiter call them when he could.

"Did you get all that?" he asked Pete. "Russell Tate has taken a loan out on Wally's house. I guess Jupiter was right to be suspicious about the haunted thermostat."

"That's terrible," Pete said. "These guys don't have any limits. I hate to think of José being muscled by creeps like this. You heard Cutter say José was scared of Slade and Russell. I bet he wants nothing more than to get out of this pickle he's gotten himself into. Maybe instead of staking out his boat, we should just go and talk to him again. I can translate. José's already talked to me once today, and he was really confiding in me. Maybe we can help! But first we've got to let him know we understand his situation."

Under normal circumstances, Bob would have said that he thought they should do what Jupiter had told them to – just hang back and see what happened – but now that he knew that Russell had been stealing from his own father, he felt surprisingly angry. Bob was normally pretty shy, but with Wally, he hadn't been, and Wally hadn't sounded very happy on the phone just now.

"All right," Bob said. "Let's do it. We'll tell him we want to help him get out from under Russell's thumb. But if he's not on deck, we'll get out of sight, O.K.?"

"O.K.," Pete said – though Bob wasn't even sure he was listening. He was striding toward the *Santa María* when Bob suddenly remembered the walkie-talkies. What if Jupiter tried to call them when they were close to the boat? These walkie-talkies were great devices, but they often squawked with static when the speaker's voice came over the air, and they could seem unnaturally loud.

"Turn off your walkie-talkie," he called ahead to Pete.

"What?" Pete said, then turned back in the direction of José's boat.

Bob was wearing a pair of paratrooper boots that came up over his ankles; he hadn't known where he might wind up, and since his ankle would always be iffy after his fall a few years back, he protected it as best he could. Now he turned off his walkie-talkie and slipped it into the top of his right boot. It felt hard and reassuring out of sight like that.

Bob caught up with Pete just as he reached the *Santa María*. The deck was deserted, but suddenly Pete started calling, "¿José? ¿José? Soy yo. Pete Crenshaw," then stepped from the floating walkway onto the deck of the boat.

Oh, no, Bob thought. Pete was always so impulsive. "Pete!" he said, as quietly as possible. "Get back here!"

Bob guessed that Pete hadn't heard him, because he watched as Pete walked over to the set of steps that led down to the cabin, bent at the waist, and called "¿José? Es Pete Crenshaw. Te hablé antes." He turned and smiled at Bob.

Suddenly a man's head appeared, sticking up out of the hold. He was very brown from the sun and had a thick bristly mustache, but what Bob noticed most was how alarmed he looked. He pushed his hands against the air in the universal signal for *Get away from me.*

"Vete, vete," he said, "¿Qué estás haciendo aquí?"

Pete turned to Bob and said, "This is José. He wants to know what I'm doing here," just as another head appeared in the hatchway. This one belonged to Russell Tate. He was wearing a black fedora, and he had a thin smile on his face that might have indicated pleasure in the sudden company if Bob hadn't known what he knew. Weren't he and Pete supposed to be watching the boat in case Russell and Slade arrived? What were they doing here already? Bob suddenly felt sick.

"Whoa!" Pete said, taking a couple of steps back. Bob had the impulse to run for it, and then stopped himself, firmly. He'd never leave Pete or Jupiter, and after all, even if this guy *was* a crook when it came to money, he was still Walter Tate's son.

As if he had all the time in the world, Russell mounted the steps to the deck. The first time Bob had met him − the day they'd gone to look at the capybaras − Bob hadn't seen his face straight on, so when Jupiter had said afterwards that the look Russell had cast in Slade's direction was the look of a boss making sure his overseer was on the job, Bob hadn't been sure he was actually right.

Now he was, because a third head appeared in the hatchway – shaped like a bullet and bald – and Russell turned to it with a cool, appraising look. Slade DeMarco was wearing a sleeveless blue t-shirt and in his right hand he held a hefty dumbbell with which he was doing bicep curls. Obviously Pete and Bob had interrupted his exercise routine.

Now he joined Russell as José moved off to one side. Slade's eyes narrowed when he saw the boys.

"Hey! Those are the kids that stole the birds!" he said.

Quick as a snake, he dropped the dumbbell, took a step forward, and grabbed Pete by the shoulders. He turned him around and hustled him down the steps and into the hold. This alarmed Bob so much he froze. Pete would normally have put up a fight, but he'd been caught so totally off guard he hadn't had time to gather himself.

Astounded at the turn of events, Bob could only conclude that Russell had given Slade a secret command of some sort and turned to look at Russell questioningly.

"You'll have to forgive my friend," Russell said, "but he was deeply upset when the four hyacinth macaws in my father's barn went missing, and he's known for a while that your friend's uncle wasn't *really* a tall, thin guy with blue-rimmed glasses."

He chuckled mock-kindly. "Luckily, Jupiter – as I believe the head of your enterprise is called – gave my father his card, and my father gave it to me."

Bob knew that Walter Tate had done no such thing, but he tried to look as if he believed it. Russell smiled thinly again, then added, "Are you Bob Andrews? You look like Records and Research, and as long as you're here, we should have a talk about those macaws."

Bob had already made his mind up not to leave Pete, so he nodded, stepped onto the deck of the *Santa María*, and approached Russell Tate, who looked down at him from his superior height. He was six foot three or four. He made a theatrical gesture of welcome, sweeping his hand toward the cabin.

"After you," he said, with exaggerated politeness.

Bob walked down the stairs, and when he reached the bottom, he found Pete struggling, trying to get away from Slade. Behind them were four medium-sized plastic kennels with wheels on the bottom and a handle on either side on the top. In each of them, a hopeful young capybara peered out through the wire mesh of the front door.

On a side table by the galley, Bob glimpsed what looked like several sizable packets of fifty-dollar bills – and he thought he knew exactly where they had come from, and who they really belonged to.

Somehow, Russell and Slade had met Jack Cutter at the warehouse, loaded and transported the capybaras to the pier, then carried them down into the *Santa María's* hold while he and Pete had been eating sandwiches and watching the waves roll in.

"You'd better let us go," Pete said as he struggled with Slade. "Our friend Rafael Solacers knows where we are, and he'll be coming to look for us if he finds we're missing. You'll be sorry."

Oh, no, Bob thought. He wanted to tell Pete to be quiet, but it was too late – the damage was already done – and now Bob was afraid that he and Pete were the ones who were going to be sorry.

Pete stopped struggling, but Slade wouldn't let him go. Bob thought about taking a run at Slade to see if Pete could get free, but Russell was standing beside him, and Bob knew there was no way he and Pete could hope to overpower these two grown men.

As far as Bob could tell, the news about Rafael had taken Russell aback. For a moment, the mask slipped and he looked worried, but then he gathered himself together and grinned.

"You mean Obi-Wan Kenobi has taken you under his wing? Well, gosh, I was going to let you off with a warning, but now that I know Rafael is up to his usual tricks, I think we should have our chat about the macaws somewhere else. We'll find a quiet corner of the ocean and see what kind of agreement we can come to. José, start the engine. Slade, untie the mooring rope and cast off."

José looked at him blankly, responding to the sound of his name. Russell jerked his chin toward the deck and said, *"Enciende el motor. We're all going for a boat ride."*

José nodded and clambered upwards, followed by Slade. Bob had a nervous side and it suddenly took over. What would his parents say if they found he'd been kidnapped? He knew he wasn't entirely equipped for moments like this. When José had backed the ketch out of the slip, turned the bow seaward, and headed the *Santa María* out into the Pacific —

presumably toward the Channel Islands — Slade returned below deck with the dumbbell he'd dropped earlier.

This was the second time in a single day that Bob had been aboard a sea-going vessel, and he'd liked the earlier trip considerably more. He didn't know what his face betrayed, but he felt pretty frightened. He had no idea where they were headed, and the combination of Russell Tate and Slade DeMarco filled him with dread.

He looked at Pete, who had achieved a modicum of calm, but who was still obviously considering the situation in terms of action. Slade had started curling the dumbbell he'd retrieved, as though now seemed as good a time as any to keep his biceps in order.

Russell looked at him and said, "You'd better save the rest of your workout for later on this evening."

He turned to Pete and Bob. "So where are the hyacinth macaws hiding out?"

Pete said, "We're not going to tell you."

"Oh, yes, you will," said Slade. "But in the meantime, I'm going to tie you up, so you can't cause any trouble."

"I'm sure that won't be necessary," Russell said. "Just stay with our young friends here while I go talk to the Mexican."

He nodded in what he seemed to think was a friendly manner, then went to join José.

Pete looked at Bob and jerked his head as though now was their chance. But what were they going to do? Run up on deck and jump overboard? Where, exactly, would that get them? Although Slade had stopped doing curls when Russell had asked him to, he hadn't put down the dumbbell, and now he started doing curls again. When one of the capybaras made an inquisitive snort, he said, "Shut up, pig!" but Pete and Bob both went over to look at it through the metal grate on the front of its kennel.

Before Bob could stop him, Pete unhooked the door to stick his hand in and pet the capybara's nose, and, as if it had been waiting for this to happen, the capybara immediately pushed past him. It didn't dart around the cabin or do anything aggressive – just left the confines of its cage, and stood looking optimistic, while Pete petted its nose and flanks.

Slade, however, seemed unmanned by being in such close quarters with what he undoubtedly thought of as a "wild animal." Holding his dumbbell like a weapon, he backed away, saying, "Get that thing back in its cage right now!"

"All right, calm down," Pete said, putting his arms around the young capybara's neck and urging it to reverse direction.

"You do know capybaras are herbivores? And that these are really young ones?" Bob added.

He knew as soon as he'd said it that this comment had been a mistake, because even though it was easy to get the bashful young capybara back into its cage, the same couldn't be said for Slade's bold and well-developed temper.

"All right!" he roared. "I've had just about enough of the two of you. You had your chance and you blew it. I don't care what Russell says! I'm going to tie you up so you can't do anything else!"

Slade went to a cupboard in the hold, found a rope, and then grabbed Pete. Bob could see that Pete was taken aback again by the ferocity of Slade's approach, and soon he was sitting with his hands tied behind him and the rope fastened to a metal bar in the counter to the left of the small propane stove.

While Slade's attention was fixed on this process, Bob calmed himself and focused his mind. He thought of slipping his cellphone out of his pocket and placing it in his left boot, but decided against it. At some point, Slade or Russell was going to search their stuff, and if they found Bob's cellphone as well as Pete's walkie-talkie, it was less likely they'd look for a second walkie-talkie.

Soon enough, Slade was tying Bob up, too. He tried to be as resigned as possible, though the instinct to fight was strong. After all, the desire for liberty was innate in all living beings. He thought of how happy the young capybara had been to get out of its cage, and that one of the reasons it could be upsetting to see animals caged was that they, too, wanted freedom.

When they'd talked, Bob's mother had said very clearly that although human beings had evolved as predators and had a powerful evolutionary instinct to think of other animals as their prey, they had also evolved to feel empathy. In the last hundred years, the empathy which had originally been directed mostly toward other human beings had finally gotten directed at other animals, too.

Remembering this conversation with his mother helped Bob keep calm at a moment when he himself was being roughly handled. And not just roughly handled, but by someone

Bob thought had to be called a thoroughgoing predator – one in whom the instinct for empathy seemed to have been permanently damaged. When Bob, too, was sitting with his hands tied behind him, Slade surveyed his work. "That's more like it. That's where the two of you *should* be. In the galley with the other perishables!"

Slade's use of "perishables" was cleverer than Bob would have expected, but after a moment of panic, he took deep breaths and looked at the kennels containing the capybaras. Bob thought the fate that awaited them – as companions of human beings who wanted them to be happy – would almost certainly be better than the one which would have awaited them in the wild, but even so, as he sat twisting his hands behind him, he had the thought that maybe they'd prefer a short life in their natural environment than a long life in a foreign one. But no one was asking them.

At that moment, Russell returned, and when he saw what Slade had done, he said in a tight, taut tone, "I thought I told you just to keep them company."

"They let one of those pigs out of its cage!" Slade said, snarling. "I told you they'd be trouble. They're going to be more trouble if we don't keep them tied up."

For a moment Bob hoped that Russell was going to tell Slade to release them, anyway, but instead, he nodded. "We'll see how it goes," he said. "For now, we need to get the capybaras up on deck. There's not enough room for all of us in here."

Russell grabbed one of the kennels by its handles, holding it crossways in front of his body, then heaved it up the stairs ahead of him. Slade followed – after which the two returned for the second set of kennels. As Slade got to the stairs, he tilted his end and the capybara inside squealed in terror.

"Shut up," Slade said ferociously to the cage he was carrying. Then he and Russell were up the stairs, disappearing from view.

Pete was incensed. "It's bad enough that he's trying to scare us," he fumed. "But why does he have to scare the capybaras?"

"Because he's a bully and a coward," Bob said.

Soon, Russell and Slade stomped down the stairs again. When they got back, Slade crossed his arms on his chest and looked at Pete and Bob. Both of their backpacks were on the floor, and Russell touched them with the toe of his boot. "Search them," he said. "And pat the kids down."

He stood watching as Slade rummaged around inside the backpacks. From an outside pocket in Pete's, Slade pulled Pete's walkie-talkie, and from Bob's pocket he took the cell-phone.

"Shall I chuck these overboard?" he asked.

"We'll return the devices when the time comes," Russell said. "We're not thieves."

Bob thought this was pretty funny, coming from Russell. But it was reassuring as well. If Russell planned to return them, there had to be someone to return them to.

Just then, like a jolt of sudden and intense electricity, Jupiter's voice came over Pete's walkie-talkie, and Bob remembered that Pete really hadn't listened when Bob had told him earlier to turn it off.

"Second? Records?" Jupiter said. "Are you there? Come in, please. Over."

Russell looked amused and seemed to be deciding whether to push the button and respond, but decided against it.

"Pete?" Jupiter said again. "Bob? Come in, please. Over." For some reason he didn't release the TALK button, and so they all heard him say, "They don't seem to be hearing me. I can't understand. The range is certainly short enough. I'll try again when we get closer to the marina."

Russell shut Pete's walkie-talkie off, then slipped both it and Bob's cellphone into a pocket of his jacket. Bob was flooded with relief that Jupiter hadn't mentioned the two walkie-talkies.

He was also glad to know that, however far the *Santa María* had traveled away from shore, there was no problem with the range. He felt sure that when Jupiter, Mallory, and Rafael got to the marina and found the *Santa María* gone, and Bob and Pete nowhere to be found, they'd reach the proper conclusion and come after them. Even so, he hoped he'd be able to contact them on his walkie-talkie somehow.

By now, the sun was starting to move toward the horizon, and although Bob could still see gold glinting on the water outside the cabin windows, he knew it would be dark before too long. He was glad that he and Pete had eaten, because he didn't think they were going to be offered dinner any time soon – although Slade was now rooting around in the galley to get some crackers and cheese, some glasses, and a bottle of tequila.

"I'd offer you something to eat," he said, "but I noticed you're both kind of tied up at the moment."

Slade poured the tequila into two glasses, handed one to Russell, then took a hefty drink. Bob felt that keeping silent wasn't the best approach in this situation; someone needed to challenge Russell. He decided it would be him.

"What's that money for?" he asked, nodding in the direction of the piles of fifty-dollar bills on the galley table. "Where did you get it?"

Russell drank some tequila and looked at Bob with an amused smile. "I really don't think my business is any of your business, do you? Suffice it to say that I'm planning to buy a boat – this one – if my plans work out."

"José wants to sell his boat?" Pete asked. "I don't think so."

"What you think is immaterial," Russell said. "There's a lot of money to be made between here and South America and José is as greedy as the next guy." He took another sip of tequila, looked at Slade, and winked.

13

Halfway To Freedom

Sitting next to Bob in the cabin of the *Santa María*, Pete was kicking himself. Why hadn't he listened to what Jupiter had told him? Why had he raced onto the deck and called down into the cabin like that? Why hadn't he done what he was certain Jupiter would have done – stay out of trouble and out of sight? He'd acted like a lunatic and had gotten both himself and Bob in hot water. Or maybe the water would be cold. Cold and salty.

He'd long ago noticed the stacks of fifty-dollar bills lying out in the open – more money than he'd seen since The Three Investigators had uncovered two million counterfeit dollars earlier in the summer in Jackson.

Still, Pete thought they had more important worries at the moment, and he was surprised when Bob suddenly asked Russell Tate what the money was for and where it had come from. The questions seemed likely to annoy Russell – something Pete thought was probably a bad idea

On the other hand, maybe Bob just

wanted to get Russell talking. Jupiter had often told both of them that almost anyone would reveal something they didn't intend to if you could just keep them talking. But as he listened, Russell's insinuation that José was eager to sell his boat was too much for Pete to take. When he'd talked to José that afternoon, José had told him that he'd inherited both the boat and Rojo from his uncle, and Pete was sure that even though he'd felt he had to give up Rojo, he'd do almost anything to hang onto the *Santa María*.

"He isn't greedy!" Pete said, in response to Russell's last remark. "But I bet his boat is worth more money than you've got over there." He gestured with his chin in the direction of the cash.

"Oh, I don't know," drawled Russell, taking another drink. "That's quite a bit of cash. José is used to nasty Mexican pesos, and when he sees all these nice American greenbacks, do you really think he'll try to bargain for something more? Did you know that these days it takes twenty Mexican pesos to make even one American dollar?"

Anger surged through Pete, and he strained at the rope tied to his wrists. To his surprise, he was able to move slightly toward Russell – who thankfully didn't notice. In fact, he got to his feet, gathered together the piles of fifties, stuck them into a blue plastic pouch with a zippered top, then thrust them into a jacket pocket.

"It's getting dark," he said to Slade. "I'm going up to consult with our Mexican friend again. You'd better come with me. And bring the bottle of tequila."

"Abso-frickin-lootley," Slade said, grinning malevolently at Pete and Bob. "I don't think they'll be going anywhere – though when they do, it won't be any place they'll need money."

A shiver ran down Pete's spine. That was the second crack Slade had made about Pete and Bob's tenuous situation.

"Boy," Pete said to Bob the minute Slade was gone. "That guy's as bad as André Laurent." Laurent was the counterfeiter who had held Pete hostage earlier in the summer.

"At least he hasn't held a knife to your throat," Bob said.

"Not yet," Pete said. "Though he looked like he wanted to."

"We just have to keep calm," Bob said. "I'm sure that Jupiter, Mallory, and Rafael are on our trail by now. As soon as they figured out what had happened, they probably took off after us. And the great thing is that I still have my walkie-talkie. Before we got on board, I put it in my boot. If I can get my hands loose, we'll be able to contact the others and tell them what's up."

"But by now they must already know!" Pete said.

"We can give them the details," Bob said. "Also, I think that box in the corner contains a deck of signal flags. My father was a Boy Scout, and when I was a kid he gave me a handbook he used to study for the Signs, Signals, and Codes Merit Badge. It contained the International Code of Signals."

"What's that?" Pete asked.

"Flags," Bob said. "Ships use them to communicate with one another. The box is sure to have a universal distress flag, and I remember what the flags for "I need a pilot" and "I need assistance" look like. If we can get those three and hang them out the window at the top of the cabin, then as soon as dawn comes, anyone who sees them will know to approach and board the *Santa María*."

Pete was filled with admiration.

"Wow!" he said. "That's terrific! If I had

to get kidnapped, I'm glad it was with you –
and wait until Jupe hears about you putting the
walkie-talkie in your boot!

"And guess what?" he added. "When
Russell said that thing about Mexican pesos, I
tried to get at him, and I can actually move
quite a lot! Slade's so dumb he tied me to
a drawer handle. Maybe I can bend over and
use my teeth to untie you, if I can get
my mouth down there."

Bob wrestled with the ropes holding him
and found that Slade hadn't been dumb twice.
He didn't have much wiggle room.

"Don't pull too hard," Pete warned him,
"or you'll just make the knots tighter
and harder to untie."

When Bob had stretched the rope as far
he could and turned his back to Pete, Pete saw
that it really might be possible. He yanked hard
to pull the drawer out, sidled over as close as
he could to Bob, then strained and bent at the
waist. He got closer and closer to the knots
keeping Bob captive until he couldn't get any
closer. Frustration shot through him. Only a
few more inches!

He straightened up. "I'll try again in a
minute," he said. "Relax." The next time he
tried, he managed to gain those extra inches,

and his teeth gripped one of the strands of the knot holding Bob's hands.

"Don't bite me!" Bob said.

Pete almost started laughing. "That's the least of our troubles," he said. He gripped the rope as strongly as he could, clenching his teeth, and slowly began to pull. There was silence in the cabin except for Pete's harsh breathing and his occasional grunts as he kept straining at the knot. His teeth ached. Could you pull your teeth right out of their sockets? Still, what else could he do? He grabbed the rope one last time and pulled with all the strength he had in his neck. He was amazed to feel it begin to pull free.

"It feels like you're making real progress!" Bob said excitedly.

"I am," Pete said. "Try that."

He'd managed to loosen the knot further and he straightened back up with a groan. His knees and back hurt a lot. But he was overjoyed to see Bob's wrists begin to pull apart and then to come free of the rope altogether.

In a flash Bob had untied Pete and they both stood there rubbing their wrists and trying to restore circulation.

"Quick," Bob said. "Fasten loops with the rope so you can slip in and out of it and we can look like we're still tied up when they get back."

As Pete was doing that, Bob rushed over to the box he'd mentioned before.

"Great!" he said, pulling out a square red flag with a big black square next to a big black circle. "This is the universal distress signal flag," he said.

He rummaged around and came up with two more. One was a big red X on a square white flag and the other was a square flag made up of a series of vertical yellow and blue stripes. The flags were made of thin strong nylon, with grommets on each end so they could be quickly snapped to the halyard and run up the mast.

Pete retrieved his pocket knife and some parachute cord, then cut off three short lengths. On the deck up above them he could hear Slade and Russell talking and laughing and drinking, so while Bob unlaced his boot and dug out his walkie-talkie, Pete tied the three flags one to the other, then hopped up on the counter and cranked open the window on the far side of the boat.

By now, night had fallen, but as he looked out the narrow windows at the world, Pete was amazed at how blue and shimmery it looked. In the small patch of sky he could see from his current vantage point, the stars were starting to come out, and as he carefully dropped the three flags down the ketch's side, Pete saw a shooting star zip toward the horizon. He cranked the window closed, wedging the rope inside it. For good measure, he tied the rope's end onto the crank.

Across the room, Bob had turned his walkie-talkie on, and now he hit TALK. As quietly and urgently as he could, he said, "Jupiter? Come in please. It's Bob. Pete and I need your help. Talk quietly."

It took a minute, but shortly Pete heard Jupiter say, "Are you on the *Santa María*? Did Russell and Slade kidnap you? Where exactly is the boat?"

"Yes," Bob said. "Yes. And I wish I knew."

There were noises up on deck, and Pete glanced at Bob with a look of warning and fear. He put one finger to his lips.

"I've got to go, Jupe," Bob said. "Don't call me back. I'll call you when I can." He shut off the walking-talkie and dropped it back in his boot.

As he scrambled down from the counter, Pete heard footsteps coming closer. He and

Bob had just enough time to slip the ropes back on their wrists when José came down the stairs. That was a surprise. Pete had been expecting the bad guys. Although José must have known that Slade had tied them up, he still looked stricken when he actually saw the boys. He slapped his hands to his cheeks.

"Lo siento," he said. "Lo siento mucho."

"What did he say?" Bob asked.

"He said he was very sorry," Pete said. "I guess about us being tied up. Or maybe about everything. I'm going to talk to him and find out as much as I can."

"Good idea," Bob said.

José had gone to the small refrigerator in the galley and had taken out a carton of eggs, a package of tortillas, a container of salsa, some chiles, and some cold cooked potatoes. He looked back and forth between the boys and the food.

"¿Estás cocinando para Russell y Slade?" Pete asked.

"Sí," José said. "Están borrachos y hambrientos."

"He said Russell and Slade are drunk and hungry," Pete told Bob. "José, queremos ayudarle."

José shook his head quickly as though he

were beyond help.

"No, no," Pete said in Spanish. "We understand. Whatever you and Cutter were doing, we know that Russell and Slade have been shaking you down and forcing you to do things you don't want to do."

José was breaking eggs into a small bowl. He glanced up and flashed a quick smile in Pete's direction. Pete figured this was all the encouragement he was going to get. But he thought if he brought up the *Santa María*, José might be more forthcoming.

"Quieren que les vendas el *Santa María*, sí?" They want you to sell your boat.

A look of despair crossed José's face. "Sí, sí," he said. "Y no lo hare. Tengo una esposa y cinco hijos, y mi velero es la cosa más valiosa que he tenido."

"He said he doesn't want to sell the boat," Pete said to Bob. "It's the most valuable thing he's ever owned."

"Ask him how this all happened," Bob said.

"¿Cómo te metiste en este problema?" Pete asked.

As he diced chiles, browned potatoes, and scrambled eggs, José told them his story. Pete interrupted him from time to time to translate the gist of what he was saying to Bob.

José lived in a small Sonoran fishing village on the Sea of Cortez. For many years all he had was a panga, a little outboard-motored fishing boat, and he had struggled to catch enough fish to support his family. But the men of his village started using gill nets to catch a fish called the totoaba – .

"The totoaba?" Bob said. "José was selling swim bladders?"

"Qué?" José said to Pete, confused by Bob's interjection.

Pete explained that Bob knew about totoabas.

"Sí," José said. "Está mal entraparlos."

"He said it's wrong to catch them," Pete said to Bob.

"Yes," Bob said.

José went on. He explained that even though it was illegal to catch them, you could make so much money that the fishermen did it anyway. But it was wrong, he said. Not just illegal but wrong. There weren't many totoaba left, and the nets the fishermen used also killed many other fish – including a rare and now-endangered porpoise. So José had decided he wouldn't do it. He looked at Bob mournfully. "El chino," he said.

"He said, 'The Chinese," Pete told Bob.

"Tell him I completely agree with him. The Chinese are wrong to do this."

"Mi amigo está de acuerdo contigo," Pete said.

A look of relief washed over José's face, and Pete could tell he'd been afraid he'd offended Bob. Pete thought that José was totally admirable for trying to figure out right and wrong in a situation as dire as the one he'd faced.

The smell of frying eggs and potatoes was interfering with Pete's ability to follow José closely – especially since he was just finishing up the cooking and had begun to talk faster. Pete had to concentrate really hard, and still he was afraid he might miss some of what José was saying.

When he'd inherited the boat from his uncle, everything had been looking up. He'd been able to travel distances, to the north and south. He'd gotten the idea from what the other fishermen were doing of exporting valuable items to a foreign market, and thought he could find something people in California might want but that wasn't scarce.

Through friends of friends, he'd hooked up with a former drug dealer-gone-straight on the coast of Colombia – just south of Panama – who was importing capybaras to Pennsylvania and Texas, and José had fallen in love with the animals and thought he might give them a try.

Everything had gone very well with him and Jack Cutter until Russell Tate and Slade DeMarco had appeared. José and Cutter had been struggling to find a way to get out from under Russell's thumb, when the plan to import the hyacinth macaws had been hatched. José thought it was also wrong, but it had one benefit. When his share of the birds was sold, he would have almost forty thousand American dollars – enough to set him and his family up for a very long time, as long as he kept the *Santa María*. The idea that Russell was trying to take it from him made him frantic.

Bob had been listening carefully, as if he understood the Spanish José was hurriedly speaking, but Pete knew that wasn't true. He summarized what José had told him in as few words as possible.

"So this trip with the hyacinth macaws was supposed to be José's first and last," he said. "He was getting out of animal smuggling completely after this trip."

José got out two tin plates and filled

them with eggs, potatoes, salsa, and tortillas. With one in each hand, he paused in front of Pete and Bob.

"Lo siento," he said again, very sadly. "Nunca pensé en contrabandear seres humanos."

He walked up the steps to the deck. "He just said he was sorry again, and that he never thought he'd ever wind up smuggling people," Pete said.

"Boy," Bob said. "I feel sorry for him. Did you see how dejected he looked?"

"Oh geez," Pete said. "I forgot to ask him where we were going! This afternoon he mentioned a harbor where he always stops but he never told me the name."

Voices filtered down from the deck where Russell and Slade were eating with great enjoyment what José had just prepared. Pete and Bob talked quietly about what they'd learned, and Bob agreed that José had gotten trapped partly because he was trying to act well. Pete urged Bob to get out the walkie-talkie and call Jupiter again, but Bob said there was no reason to do that until they had a better sense of where they were going.

For quite a long while, nothing much happened. From time to time, Pete and Bob talked a bit, but for the moment, they were stuck between past and future – halfway to freedom, but still trapped. It was good to be able to move around the cabin when they wanted, but although Pete thought of eating some cheese and crackers, he really didn't dare to. They'd been traveling at an amazingly brisk pace for well over five hours now, but even though it was late in the evening – almost the next morning – the ketch showed no signs of stopping for the night.

All of a sudden, there were voices on deck and the sound of footsteps about to descend the stairs.

"If Slade and Russell are coming back down, let's pretend we're asleep!" Pete said.

They slumped and closed their eyes just in time. Russell and Slade stumbled down the stairs. Each of them held a glass in one hand and Russell had the empty tequila bottle in the other. They were laughing. When Russell saw Pete and Bob, he made exaggerated shushing noises.

"They're sleeping," he whispered. "My mother always said I was so good when I was sleeping."

For some reason this made Slade laugh really hard.

"You sure can get José worked up," Russell said. "Why'd you tell him you were thinking of letting the rodents loose on the island when we get there?"

"Because I knew it would get him worked up," Slade said.

Both of them were slurring their words a bit, but they didn't seem so drunk that they were incapacitated.

"He cares about those animals like they're his kids," Slade sneered. "And I *would* let them out, but they stink so bad."

"Except they're a paycheck," Russell said. "And I don't think they'd do very well there. They like swampy conditions, not dry, rocky, salty conditions. But they wouldn't be the first non-indigenous species. I mean, other than tourists and conservationists."

Russell thought that was funnier than Slade did.

"What are you talking about?" Slade asked him.

"There's a herd of bison on the island," Russell said. "My overeducated father told me they filmed a western there in the 1920s and they imported a herd of bison. When they wrapped, the film company didn't want to pay to ship them back to the mainland, so they just left them! Now there's a herd of a couple of hundred."

Russell thought this was pretty amusing.

Pete opened his eyes just a little. Slade had propped himself in a chair on the opposite side of the cabin. Russell had found a bottle of something else and had tipped a little into their glasses.

"But about the boat," he said. "We need to do this pronto. We give him maybe ten grand max, and then we resell it for fifty or sixty. And then we'll buy something with a big fast set of motors – something better set up for the sort of operation we have in mind. And no more capybaras, either. They're too big and there's not enough money in them."

"So it's just the little tweety birds?" Slade said

"Abso-frickin-lootley," Russell spat out. "Hyacinth macaws are great. So are toucans. And palm cockatoos. They're all worth more than the rodents. And we ought to start looking into monkeys. I heard a chimpanzee can fetch sixty grand."

"How do we unload them?" Slade said.

"We'll work that out," Russell said. "We'll keep Cutter around until we figure out his network. Then we'll ditch him. I've got plenty of seed money from the so-called home improvement loan. We'll buy a warehouse so we don't have to rent some shabby place like the one Cutter got us — something more private, somewhere on the coast."

Pete felt a fire slowly building in his chest. Russell really *was* stealing from his father, a man in his nineties who'd fought in World War II, and who'd just lost his wife. Pete was outraged, but he had to continue pretending to be asleep.

"What are we gonna do about these two?" Slade said. The capybaras were on deck, so Pete knew Slade was talking about him and Bob — and suddenly Russell sounded almost sober.

"I don't know," he said harshly. "We never should have brought them with us. Damn Rafael Solares. I lost my head when the kid mentioned he was nearby."

"Why not just dump them overboard?" Slade said. "Maybe a whale will get them."

"Whales don't eat people," Russell said. "And I don't really want to hurt the kids. I just want them to get amnesia or something. I wonder if we could drug them? Aren't there drugs that can make you lose your memories?"

"Yeah," Slade chuckled. "Like every single one."

Pete didn't think Slade's remark was funny. In fact, taken with everything else that had been happening, it made him so angry that he could hardly keep himself from jumping to his feet and rushing this pair of loons. However, after a while, they climbed back up the stairs to the deck of the *Santa María,* taking their bottle of liquor and a couple of quilts and blankets with them.

14

Two Harbors

On the gently rolling deck of the *Rainbow Bridge*, Jupiter stared out at the moonlit ocean. It had been about a half an hour since both his and Mallory's walkie-talkies had crackled into life, and, suddenly, out of the darkness, they'd heard Bob's voice saying "Jupiter? Come in, please. It's Bob. Pete and I need your help. Talk quietly."

At the time this happened, Mallory had been sitting in the bow of the boat, but as soon as she'd heard Bob's voice, she'd hurried to join him and Rafael in the stern. It had taken Jupiter a fairly long minute to pull his walkie-talkie out of his pocket, hit the TALK button, and respond, and during that minute he'd had time to gather his thoughts. So he'd been able to be concise with his questions. "Bob," he'd asked. "Are you on the *Santa María*? Did Russell and Slade kidnap you? Where exactly is the boat?"

"Yes, yes, and I wish I knew," Bob had responded, and the form of his answer, as much as its content, had told Jupiter that Bob and Pete were basically all right. Otherwise it would have been harder for Bob to answer Jupiter's questions as concisely as he had asked them.

Even so, ever since Bob had said, "Don't call me back. I'll call you when I can," Jupiter had been thinking of little but Bob and Pete. More accurately, he'd been using the information he'd received during that brief contact to try to deduce what had happened so far, and the only thing he was sure of was that Bob had lost his cellphone – or had it taken away – or he would have used it to call Rafael.

After all, although walkie-talkies were terrific in certain situations, when there were people nearby who might threaten you, a cellphone was a safer bet. You still had to keep your voice down to try to avoid being overheard, but you could set the phone to vibrate and you could keep the phone to your head, so you could take an incoming call if you had to.

One question, then, was: If Bob had had his cellphone taken away, why did he still have his walkie-talkie? Putting that aside, Jupiter next considered the question of why Russell and Slade had kidnapped Pete and Bob to begin with.

As he considered this second question,

Rafael said, "Jupiter, do you mind taking the wheel for a moment? I need to grab those charts and look for one I made some notes on. All you need to do is keep your hands at nine and three o'clock and hold firm."

He grabbed a flashlight and the charts and took them into the bow where he could spread them out and look at them carefully.

Jupiter had never been at the wheel of a boat like this one before, and he was eager to see what it felt like. The wind was steady from the south, the moon was high in the sky, the heavens were spangled with stars. Sitting near the railing, Mallory was silent, staring up at the sky with a rapt expression.

Jupiter could see her plainly in the moonlight. She had pulled her legs up toward her and had wrapped her arms around them, resting her cheek against her knees. She looked smart and alert, as always, and with Pete and Bob in danger together, he was glad she was with him. She was solid.

They'd been stumped up in Auburn in their search for the map that would lead them to Li Chang's gold, but Mallory had seen what was hiding in plain sight, and because of her, not only had they been able to find the gold for Isabella Chang but had also been rewarded with enough money to buy the Flex. When none of the three of them could have posed as a history fan to coax a copy of the forged Kit Carson letter from Daniel Hernández, Mallory had been there and had risen to the occasion. And in the case at the Rocky Beach Summer Theatre Festival, she had not only provided crucial information from her own realm of knowledge but had taken the initiative to solve one of the case's central mysteries by making a trans-Atlantic phone call.

Jupiter marveled as he thought of her winning combination of persistence and tact, and her preternatural ability to be in the right place at the right time. Over the course of two months, she'd been smart, brave, resilient, resourceful, and patient; she'd bided her time; she'd never been pushy or antagonistic. She'd been great. Over the last few weeks, Jupiter had felt his resolve and resistance begin to loosen and then to crumble.

He was glad to know her.

On this case, it had been she who helped identify the sound of the carillon, which had brought them to José's boat. Now that he thought about it, if they hadn't found José's boat, Pete and Bob would not now be on it, in the clutches of Russell Tate. But he could hardly blame Mallory for that.

"I hope Bob calls again soon," Mallory said suddenly. "It's frustrating not being able to call him."

"Yes, it is," Jupiter said. "But that frustration is worth it if it keeps the walkie-talkie from being discovered. Without it, we'd be completely cut off."

Mallory lifted her head. "Do you really think they're in danger?"

"Anything can happen," Jupiter said, "but I don't think Russell Tate wants to move from smuggling animals to killing people."

Mallory nodded and looked back up at the sky, while Jupiter turned his own attention to his task. He was concentrating so hard that he was almost startled when Rafael set the charts down and casually took the wheel back.

"See?" Rafael. "You didn't steer us off the edge of the world. I couldn't find the one I was looking for, but it may be useful to have these charts, anyway."

Jupiter went to sit next to Mallory – not right next to her, but nearby. Rafael kept heading south. The air was light and sweet and cool and smelled faintly of brine. Time passed – what seemed like a *lot* of time – and then suddenly, Jupiter's walkie-talkie crackled again. Only when he heard the noise did he realize he'd actually been asleep. He pulled the walkie-talkie from his pocket. Even though he was expecting to hear it, when Bob's voice leapt across the ocean, magnified by the walkie-talkie, Jupiter practically jumped.

He had a hundred questions he wanted the answers to, but he realized that now was not the time to ask them, so he waited as patiently as he could for Bob to finish. It was a relief to hear his voice.

"We've stopped for the night," Bob said. "Everything's pretty quiet. We're in some harbor. Definitely not in a marina. José dropped anchor. I guess Russell doesn't want to get too close to shore."

"Is Pete with you?" Jupiter asked.

"He's up on deck," Bob said. "Russell is making him translate. Russell speaks a little Spanish, but he isn't as fluent as Pete, and he's trying to get José to sell the *Santa María* to him. José doesn't want to sell it at all, and he especially doesn't want to sell it for a fraction of what it's worth."

"I'd love to hear Pete's translation," Jupiter said wryly.

"Me, too," Bob said. "We can bet he's not doing it word-for-word. I'm actually glad this has happened, because as long as Pete is up on deck with Slade and Russell, they won't be coming down to the cabin. I've got a lot to tell you. Wally Tate called me on my cellphone when I was still in Isla Vista."

"He tried to call Rafael, too," Jupiter said. "What did he say?"

"He discovered that Russell used a Power of Attorney Wally had given him to take a loan out on his house. You were right that Russell was trying to push Wally out with that haunted thermostat routine. I think he must have wanted to get an appraiser in so that he could get a home equity loan, or something.

"I also think he must have gotten an advance on it – which he's trying to use to buy the *Santa María*. He plans to resell it for fifty thousand dollars more than he pays José, then use the profit and the home equity loan to buy a boat and a warehouse to get into animal smuggling in a much bigger way. But I think he's finally realized that he made a mistake in kidnapping me and Pete."

Jupiter wished he had time to digest all this properly, but he knew that Russell and Slade might be interrupting Bob at any moment.

"Are you in immediate danger?" he

asked. "If so, we need to call the Coast Guard."

"Russell and Slade drank a bottle of tequila," Bob said. "I think we'll be fine for the night. Also, Pete is determined to make sure José doesn't get arrested, or deported, or lose his boat. The reason he's been smuggling capybaras to California was because his other basic alternative was to get into gill-netting the totoaba fish. You know, the one with the air bladders the Chinese use to make fish maw soup?"

"I understand," said Jupiter. He did, too. Pete hated the idea of José getting punished for making an ethical decision – and all because men like Russell didn't know what ethical decisions were.

"Do you know where you are yet?" Jupiter asked. He and Mallory were hunched over the walkie-talkie so they wouldn't miss a word.

"No," Bob said, "but I can tell you what I see out the cabin window. There are a good number of other boats at anchor – mostly sailboats, some big ones. They're all shut up for the night. I can see a little stretch of land, with what looks like another harbor on the other side, and a small village. Mountains on both sides of the isthmus."

Jupiter thought this was quite a lot to go on. At the wheel, Rafael was listening carefully when Jupiter asked, "Is there anything else you can tell us?"

"I don't know if this will help, but I heard Russell telling Slade there's a herd of bison on the island – left over from some western they shot here in the 1920s."

"They're in Catalina Harbor on Santa Catalina," Rafael said without hesitation. "It's the only island with bison. The town he's seeing is called Two Harbors."

"Did you hear that, Bob?" Jupiter asked.

"Yes," Bob said.

"I know exactly where it is," Rafael said. "We can be there in an hour."

A wave of relief washed over Jupiter. He could only imagine how Bob must be feeling. When you were chasing after someone, it was always good to know where they were – and even more so if you were the one being chased and you wanted to be found!

"We'll be expecting you," Bob said. "I better get off now. Oh, but when you get here, I think you should wait until dawn to approach the boat. There's no way it's going anywhere again until then."

"Wait!" Jupiter said. "How will we know

it's you in the dark? You said there are a lot of sailboats."

"Pete hung three distress flags out the cabin window," Bob said. "You'll see them clearly in the moonlight. They're on the starboard side."

"Good work, Records," Jupiter said. "See you soon. Over."

Great! he thought. Pete and Bob had been taking good care of themselves.

Rafael had put the engines on idle while Bob and Jupiter were talking, but now he revved them up and soon they were skimming over the waters again, in a slightly different direction, straight for Santa Catalina Island.

"I haven't been to Cat Harbor in a while," Rafael told Jupiter and Mallory, "but Santa Catalina is a great island – if all you're doing is hiking and picnicking and not worrying about rescuing your friends. There's good whale-watching off the coast to the west, and in the summer you can see humpbacks as well as gray and blue whales."

"Maybe some other time," Jupiter said. "I'll be busy Bob-and-Pete-watching."

Mallory laughed.

"Remember that carving of the humpback you gave me, Jupiter?" Rafael asked.

"The one my friend did that was in the box your uncle bought at Wally's? He carved that using a piece of driftwood he found on Santa Catalina. Our people inhabited those islands in the long ago."

Jupiter did remember. The whale was beautifully carved, its long body sinuously curving into the raised tail and flukes of a whale about to slap the water. He imagined the explosion of spray rising into the sky and hanging there as stars. It was a glorious night, and now that he knew where his friends were, all seemed well again. Out in the distance, something glinted in the moonlight – something that looked like an island peeking its head above water and then submerging. For all Jupiter knew, it could be a humpback breaching.

Suddenly Jupiter found himself saying to Rafael and Mallory, "I've been thinking about what Bob said about Pete not wanting José to get into the hands of the authorities, and I have to say that I agree with him."

"I do, too," said Mallory.

Rafael nodded. "You don't need to convince me," he said. "From what we've heard, José was never trying to hurt anybody. The rule of law has been important to human progress, but laws are rigid and uncompromising things;

they don't deal in nuance."

"I know what you mean," Jupiter said. He was thinking about the five counterfeit one hundred dollar bills he'd kept as a memento of the Jackson case – and how he'd bent the law just a little to keep them. "The law has no use for shades of gray."

"I look like a respectable citizen most days," Rafael said, "though my truck and my hair give some people pause. And Elena works in a lawyer's office, for heaven's sake! Even so, I have a lot of memories of times when people in positions of power abused it."

"So do I," said Mallory. "There was this woman in Scotland who was just a crossing guard at the elementary school, but boy, did she think she ruled the world. You wouldn't believe the pleasure she took in getting traffic to stop. It wasn't about keeping kids safe. It was about putting her hand up and having cars screech to a halt."

Jupiter smiled. He'd encountered plenty of officious bureaucrats in all walks of life. "It's a vexing question," he said. "According to the authorities, José broke the law and should be punished. But none of them would take the time to weigh who he really is or why he acted as he did. Justice is supposed to enforce fairness, but frequently it's just a shortcut to punishment."

"Or vengeance," Rafael said.

"But what about Russell and Slade?" Mallory asked.

"I've never met Slade," Rafael said, "but while it might seem as if Russell's the mastermind, telling Slade what to do, I actually think it's the other way around. I wouldn't be surprised if Russell weren't a little frightened of Slade. At any rate, he's clearly a bad influence."

"That could be so," Jupiter said. He remembered in their last case how Madhuri Singh had had a bad effect on Reginald Ward.

"Anyway," Rafael went on. "Russell Tate has reached a dead end. His father is wise to him now, the money supply will immediately dry up, and without any cash, whatever animal smuggling plans Russell had will vanish. As far as punishing him and Slade, I've always thought the proper question about meting out punishment was whether it would do any actual good.

"If someone is intent on mayhem, then by all means get him away from other people. But in most cases, it makes more sense to ask whether the conditions the lawbreaker was acting under have changed. With José and Cutter wanting out − and with no money, and us about to catch up with him − what's Russell going to do? He's not completely bad. And even if Slade is, without Russell to think things through for him, he'll find some other way to express his poisonous nature."

"That sounds right to me," Mallory said, and Jupiter nodded in agreement.

"As for Jack Cutter," Jupiter said. "If you could have seen him with the two dogs he met, or how well he was taking care of the macaws and capybaras in the warehouse, you'd agree with us about how much he really cares about animals. He may have been trying to game the system and make some money, but he never wanted to hurt the animals he was dealing with."

"I think we could probably persuade him to go straight," Mallory said. "When this is all over, maybe we can go to the bird shop where he works and talk sense to him. Besides, we learned that the hyacinth macaws were a one-time deal, and without José as a partner, where's he going to get capybaras?"

Jupiter glanced at Rafael who stood, his feet planted firmly, grasping the wheel with both hands. If he'd ever seen a symbol of the right kind of authority, it was Rafael Solares on the deck of the *Rainbow Bridge*, Jupiter thought. Then he yawned, a yawn so big and wide it made his jaw hurt.

Rafael looked at him and Mallory and said, "It'll be a while longer before we get to Cat Harbor. Why don't the two of you go forward and relax?"

This sounded good to Jupiter, so he and and Mallory made their way to the front of the boat. There, they grabbed some cushions off the chairs and laid them out on deck. Mallory threw back the top of her sleeping bag, crawled in, and pulled it over her. Jupiter tried to get comfortable with his jacket but didn't quite manage it.

As he tossed from one side to the other, Jupiter noticed that Mallory's breathing had become more steady. She might be asleep. It was hard to believe that she'd been a stranger at the start of the summer. He'd been suspicious of her — as he would have been of anyone who seemed more than ordinarily interested in The Three Investigators — but now she seemed not strange at all, but familiar and even safe.

It was an amazing night, Jupiter thought. Although he had always tried to balance the world of the mind with solid physical

tasks, those tasks often took place in the Salvage Yard. This was a different world entirely –
a world of wind and water, clean, fresh, bracing, wordless. Here he was, skimming the surface of the western ocean, as under him and over him water and air made a perfect circle.

Earlier that summer, in Yosemite, and then again in Auburn and Jackson, Jupiter had allowed himself to experience the world in its full glory. To sink into it, not just to rest on its surface but to understand its deep reality – to feel the truth of rocks and sun, of mountains and grapevines and caverns. Now, the ocean and the stars. The sky between those stars was black and velvety smooth, and the vast expanse overhead was breathtaking.

From reading an astronomy book recently, Jupiter knew that the distances he was looking at were so vast that some of the stars he was seeing had long since burnt out, but their light, which was taking so long to reach earth, was still shining. That was a truly startling thought, and as Jupiter lay there, thinking and looking up, he suddenly saw a shooting star streak across the heavens.

Even as he saw it, he knew it wasn't a star like the others he was looking at, but a bit of cosmic debris − a meteor heating up and burning to nothing as it entered earth's atmosphere.

Jupiter also knew that since it was early August, the Perseid meteor shower would be starting any day now, and that this might be a sort of early envoy − a single fiery raindrop in what would soon be a perfect storm of shooting stars. Jupiter had always liked shooting stars, but there was something about this one that seemed especially significant. It was the first one he'd seen since he'd met his mother's aunt and discovered that his mother and father had both been astronomers.

He was watching its afterimage when Rafael called out from the stern of the boat that he could see, in the distance, the lights of Catalina Harbor − where Pete and Bob were waiting for him and Mallory to arrive.

15

Help From The Deep

Now that Bob knew they were in Catalina Harbor on Santa Catalina Island − still in the state of California, if thirty miles from the mainland − he felt better. A lot. He could picture the map and had a vague idea of the island's position. It had been unnerving to be under someone else's control, moving unmoored over the earth's surface, without any sense of where he and Pete were heading.

He was pretty tired − not only because it was almost 2:00 in the morning, but also from all the tension and worry. Now he could relax − at least a little. Bob could see that Pete was tired, too. The fizzy energy and enthusiasm Pete usually had was gone and had been ever since he'd come below after translating − or pretending to − for Russell. When it was clear to Russell that he was making no progress with José, he'd gotten frustrated and had called the negotiations off for the time being.

Unfortunately for Bob, sleep seemed out of the question. He and Pete had faked it earlier, but Bob knew that if he stretched out and actually went to sleep, it would be clear that his hands were no longer tied. And Russell might well come back; he'd already been below once to check for more liquor in the cabinet.

On that trip to the cabin, he'd taken off his jacket and hung it in a wall cupboard – apparently forgetting, or not caring, that in one pocket were Bob's cellphone and Pete's walkie-talkie, and in the other a bag of cash. The clatter of footsteps tore Bob out of a half-doze. He looked up to see José rummaging around for food and water for the capybaras. After grabbing a bag and a plastic jug, he moved close to Pete.

"Gracias por tu ayuda," he said softly.

"De nada," Pete said. "He's thanking me for my help," he told Bob. José looked up the passageway to the deck to see if anyone was coming, and then he spoke very rapidly to Pete.

Pete shook his head. "¡Espera!" he said. "Más lentamente."

José grinned and began speaking more slowly. It was useless trying to understand, and sooner or later Bob knew Pete would tell him what José was saying. So, for the moment, he just watched Pete, who nodded when he understood, shook his head from time to time and said, "Repita, por favor." He also made appropriate – or Bob guessed they were appropriate – expressions ranging from dismay to excitement. After a long stretch of Spanish, Pete said, "Un momento, por favor," and turned to Bob.

"Wow!" Pete said. "We're almost out of gas. José says the engine is running on fumes. He usually gases up further south, and anyway, he's such a good sailor that he almost never uses the engine, but Russell thought using it instead of the sails would be safer and faster. Especially faster. Which it was.

"We got here from Isla Vista in less time than it would usually take – at least on a sailboat. On a boat like the *Rainbow Bridge*, it wouldn't take more than three hours, flat out. But José knows the currents and has a route that lets him use them. He also says that the gas gauge is broken so it looks like there's gas when there isn't. He knows from the noises the engine's making that the tank was almost empty when we got here."

"What's the problem?" Bob asked.

"José's afraid that when Russell and Slade discover we're out of gas, they're going to get angry. They're not going to want to risk gassing up in a small community where everyone knows everyone else's business. Also, he's worried about the capybaras. Usually he sets up a wire holding pen in half of the cabin and gives them the run of it. With the door to the deck closed, of course."

Bob smiled at the idea of free-range capybaras roaming the area in which he and Pete had been held captive.

"Why don't you tell him what we know?" Bob asked. "Tell him about the walkie-talkie and that our friends and the man he sold Rojo to are on their way to rescue us."

Pete translated as best he could. In the midst of the words Bob didn't understand, he heard "el walkie-talkie," which made him laugh.

"Tell him," Bob said, "that we've warned them not to approach us until daybreak, but that as soon as there's light, they'll probably board and confront Russell and Slade."

José was nodding that he understood as Pete translated, but his expression alternated between relief and worry. "No haga daño a mi velero," he said. "O los chigüires."

"He's afraid his boat or the capybaras will get hurt," Pete said.

"Tell him that won't happen if we have a

plan," Bob said.

"Excuse me for asking," Pete said, "but *do* we have a plan?"

What could they do? Bob wondered. How could they keep Russell and Slade off-guard while the others had time to board? And then it came to him. Create a distraction!

"Maybe when Jupe and the others get here, José could let the capybaras loose on deck. They'd run around and get underfoot, and while Russell isn't afraid of them, Slade definitely is."

Pete started laughing at the image of four capybaras loose on the deck of the *Santa María*. "The doors on their kennels hook on the top and bottom," Pete said. "Maybe he could unhook the tops now, and then he'd only have to do the bottoms later at the right moment."

"Great idea," Bob said. Pete explained all this to José who at first seemed a little uncertain. He shook his head and muttered "los chigüires" several times.

"He's worried about the capybaras," Pete said.

"They'll be fine on deck," Bob said. "No one will hurt them."

José listened carefully, then seemed convinced. Pete, Bob thought, could convince anyone of anything.

"Sí, sí," José said, finally nodding his head with great conviction.

"We might as well tell him everything," Bob said. "We can trust him. Explain we're just pretending to be tied up and that we'll be ready to jump into action at the right time. And tell him you put those three signal flags out the cabin window."

Pete pulled his hands from behind him and showed them to José who looked at Pete as though he'd just produced a rabbit out of a hat. "Mira," Pete said. "¡Nuestras manos están sueltos. Y colgamos banderas afuera de la ventana!"

"¡Estupendo!" José said. A big grin crossed his face. "Son muchachos buenos."

For the first time, José looked really hopeful, as if deliverance were finally at hand. Bob resolved not to let him down. José was about to go back up on deck when Bob had what he thought was a great idea.

"Maybe you should tell José to ask Russell to come down here so that we can explain what José just told us – only we won't mention the gas," he said to Pete. "We'll say that José says something is wrong with the engine, and he just noticed it as we were coming into the harbor. That it was making some sort of spluttering noise or something. Then we can tell him José thinks we'll need to get a mechanic from town to fix it."

Pete started to translate when Bob told him to stop. "Wait," he said, "I'm not done. If Russell acts the way I think he will, he'll say no way to the mechanic. Wally Tate said Slade was a really good mechanic – you can tell José that's the truth – and Russell will believe Slade can fix whatever's wrong."

"But if he's such a good mechanic," Pete said, "won't he figure out about the gas gauge?"

"We'll have to hope he doesn't," Bob said. "He's drunk, remember, and once he gets it into his head the problem's mechanical, I don't think he'll have the flexibility to think it's something as simple as the gas – especially if the gauge is reading full. The important thing is to have José get Russell down here. We'll do the talking and make sure the issue of gas never comes up. Then, whatever happens, when Russell thinks it's time to leave the harbor, he'll think the only way to go is under sail. Ask José if Russell knows anything about sailing."

Pete turned to José. "¿Sabe Russell

cómo navegar en un velero?" he asked.

José looked at Pete as though he'd lost his mind, shook his head no, and started laughing.

"That's what I thought," Bob said. "That's great. José will have total control. Once we get underway in the morning, we can rush the deck, and with the capybaras loose, Russell and Slade won't know what hit them."

"Maybe the boom will hit them!" Pete said.

"That would be perfect," Bob said. "But with Jupe and the others arriving on the *Rainbow Bridge*, we should have plenty of help."

Pete finished filling José in on all the details. He nodded and walked up on deck. It would take a little while before he sent Russell, Bob thought, because his first priority was to care for the capybaras. But it wasn't long before Russell appeared, looking heavily aggrieved.

"What's going on?" he asked. "José keeps saying 'el motor' and pointing down here."

"I guess there's a problem," Bob said. "José was just talking to Pete, telling him that the engine was making weird sputtering noises as we were coming into the harbor."

"Oh that's great," Russell said. "Just what I need."

"José thinks we should get an engine mechanic from the island when it's light out," Pete said.

"Does he?" Russell said, looking mightily offended, as if José had no right to an opinion on the matter. "Slade's a mechanic. Whatever the problem is, I'm sure he can fix it." He shook his head in disgust. "I was hoping to get some shuteye, but I can kiss that idea goodbye. I just hope José has a tool kit."

He turned and trudged back up on deck as though the weight of the world rested on his shoulders. Bob smiled at Pete, who grinned at him enthusiastically.

In the middle of the night, rocking on the gentle waves in Cat Harbor, it was very still and quiet. Bob could hear Russell's steely voice up on deck, swearing, talking heatedly to Slade, and Slade's annoyed responses.

"Yeah, yeah," Slade said, faintly. "I'm going as fast as I can."

"What's the problem?" Russell said.

"I can't get the engine cowling off," Slade said. "I don't know about marine engines. Marine mechanics have their own certification. I'm a car mechanic for frick's sake.

And this is an old motor."

"Listen," Russell said, "calm down. You're very good. I know that. You can do this."

"Yikes," Pete said. "You sure got them going." He paused as the bickering continued. "Are you as hungry as I am?" he asked.

"Starving," Bob said.

Pete went to his backpack and pulled out the bag of nuts and raisins he had packed in the Salvage Yard.

"Jupiter told me we probably wouldn't need these. Boy, was he wrong." He took a handful and threw it into his mouth, then handed the bag to Bob.

Bob closed his eyes and savored every bite. The combination of salty nuts and sweet chewy raisins was almost too good. When he was done, he said to Pete, "I'm going to check on the flags." He peered out the cabin window where the three flags hung vertically against the side of the boat. No one would see them yet, and that included Russell and Slade, he hoped.

Reassured, he was about to turn away from the window when he was struck by how beautiful everything looked. The lights in Two Harbors were a meager reflection of the millions of stars overhead – each of them, Bob knew, a blazing sun like the one at the center of the solar system.

As he watched, something caught his eye, and he looked just in time to see a bright streak shoot across the night sky, leaving a brief trail of fire in its wake. It was an incredibly gorgeous night, and an incredible place. As tired as he was, he couldn't wait for daybreak to see the place more clearly.

He turned around. Pete was still eating from the bag of nuts and raisins but more slowly now. Bob listened carefully for noises on deck from Slade and Russell, but there were none – no talking, no clanking, no swearing, no banging. He assumed that all that drinking had finally caught up with the two of them and that they were now sleeping or unconscious up on the deck.

The knowledge that nothing was about to happen anytime soon, together with the exhaustion that had swept over him, let Bob close his eyes for a moment. Briefly he fought to open them again and then gave in to the luxury of not having to do so. He slumped onto the floor and fell asleep.

When he came awake again, several hours later, he was so bleary and disoriented that for a moment he had trouble reconstructing what had happened and where he was. On the floor near him, Pete lay still asleep, and the first thing Bob did was nudge his friend with his foot.

"Wake up," Bob whispered. Pete started awake, rubbed his eyes, and sat up. He was instantly more awake, Bob could see, than he was.

Light was filtering in through the cabin windows and down the steps, and from up on deck came the sound of voices. It seemed that Russell and Slade were just waking up, too. Slade was complaining loudly of a headache.

"Russell, you jackass," he was saying. "You made me drink too much."

Russell's voice was incredulous. "I made you drink? You guzzled that stuff down like you hadn't had a drink in years."

"I think I'm going to be sick," Slade said.

"Be sure you make it to the rail," Russell said. And then his voice took on a turn of urgency bordering on hysteria. "Jeez!" he said. "It's the *Rainbow Bridge*!"

"What are you talking about?" Slade said.

"That boat!" Russell said, his voice rising. "I'd know it anywhere, with its rubber bumpers. It belongs to Rafael Solares, the guy my father knows. If it hadn't been for him, I wouldn't have left Isla Vista so fast in the first place – and never with those kids on board. He's tracked us down, somehow."

"Cool it!" Slade said. "Get a grip."

"Where's José?" Russell said. "He's got to get us out of here! Now!"

"What about the motor?" Slade said.

"What about it?" Russell said, his voice distraught. "We don't have one. José will have to sail without it. Let's help him haul up the sails."

There was a lot of banging about and shouting and then Bob could hear the ratcheting noise, as hand over hand, the mainsail and mizzen sail were raised. The wind was gentle, but as soon as the sails were raised Bob could feel the boat respond as it tugged against its anchor.

"Haul that thing up!" Russell told Slade.

The *Santa María* began to turn into the wind. José was an expert sailor, and he managed to swing the bow around to the north and to set a course that would hug the coast of Santa Catalina Island until he was clear of it and could set out into the open sea. Bob peered out the portside cabin window as the mountains on the northern end of the island glided past. He could see the mist-wreathed tip of land ahead in the brightening light.

Though José was in control and there was no motor that Russell could commandeer, Bob suddenly felt a jolt of nerves. What if Jupiter, Mallory, and Rafael, aboard the *Rainbow Bridge*, were all asleep and hadn't seen them leaving Cat Harbor? Bob had warned them about boarding before daybreak, but now he was afraid they might lose the *Santa María* entirely. And if Russell got away this time, who knew where he'd have José head the boat, or when Rafael would find them again?

When was the right time to act? Presumably José had rigged the capybaras' cages so that he'd only have to jiggle one metal hook to free them, but Bob knew José would wait until the boys joined him on deck, and, for all Bob's planning, he didn't know when the proper time to do that was.

The *Santa María's* sails had captured the wind, and the boat was sailing northwest at a good clip. Out the portside windows, Bob saw the island's tip slip past, and then all at once the Pacific opened up before them, and José adjusted the sails and turned the wheel to enter the open sea.

Hurriedly Bob conferred with Pete, and they quickly decided they didn't want to get too far from the island before they acted. It was now or never. As quietly as they could, they crept up the steps separating the cabin from the deck, Bob shushing Pete with exaggerated motions of his hands. But Pete's enthusiasm for action, which had dimmed last night, was back to full, and it was all Bob could do to keep Pete from leaping past him and up onto the deck.

They paused at the top of the stairs to see what was up. José was at the wheel, and as soon as their heads appeared, he saw them. With one hand he pointed to the bow, where Russell stood, his arms crossed, staring out to sea. Slade was crumpled over the railing.

Thin clouds scudded across the sky, and the east was a brilliant band of orange fading to peach. The mountain peaks of Santa Catalina rose stark and dark against the brightening sky, and over them light seemed to cascade until the surface of the ocean glittered. It was a glorious morning. Bob had never been out on the open ocean at daybreak before, and he knew he'd never forget it. It was like seeing the world being created before your eyes.

Pete was equally struck with wonder. Bob glanced to the south and, for a moment, he couldn't quite understand what he was seeing. Off the western coast of Catalina Island, some distance from them, it looked like the surface of the ocean was parting and a huge underwater silo was emerging. Bob reached to find a comparison – a geyser erupting, a mountain thrusting upward – but none of those quite prepared him for the sight.

A humpback whale was shooting straight up into the sky, shedding a cloak of silver water, his gigantic jaw open, his flippers dangling to either side of him. Up, up he rose, until Bob was sure that two-thirds or more of his body had appeared, and then, like a redwood slowly toppling, he turned and fell back into the water, splashing spray high into the sky. Bob looked to his right. Pete had seen it too and he stood there openmouthed.

Seeing the boys come on deck, José sprang into action. He set the wheel, then hurried to where Slade and Russell had put the capybaras' cages. Swiftly, he unhooked the latches and then darted back to the wheel. Bob watched as the long sloped brown noses of the capybaras appeared, inching their way out of the cages, hesitant at first and then with more and more confidence. When their heads had fully appeared, their eyes gleamed with excitement. Do capybaras smile? Bob wondered. He thought perhaps they did.

They began to wander freely on the deck, sticking their noses into a bucket, a pile of coiled rope. One went to the gunwales, clambered onto a box, and peered overboard to see what he could see.

Russell and Slade, too, had seen the whale breach, and they stared in its direction, gawping. It wasn't until then that the two of them noticed what had happened when they'd had their backs turned, and their reaction to seeing four loose capybaras and two loose boys on the deck was cartoon-comical. Russell's mouth flapped open and closed. Shade dragged himself back from the railing and started swearing. Russell waved his arms as though attacked by a swarm of mosquitoes and started yelling at José as though it was all his fault. They looked at one another in alarm and dismay.

What should they do? Who should they catch first? It seemed a bit much for their addled minds — a broken motor, the sudden appearance of one of Russell's sworn enemies, and now a full-scale prison break. From the look on Russell's face, Bob could see Russell thought that this just wasn't fair at all. At all.

Russell and Slade started walking swiftly down the side of the deck toward the stern. As soon as they had cleared the mainsail's mast, José spun the wheel, turning the bow to port, and the boat began to come about. The force of the wind in the sail tilted the deck, and just at that moment, on the starboard side, Bob watched in astonishment as the humpback he'd seen at a distance breached again − this time not a hundred feet from the *Santa María*.

He was absolutely gigantic, a creature of imagination, so big he blotted out the sky, and his blue-black body seemed to rise in slow motion, the inertia of his tremendous effort underwater playing out as though he were going to come entirely out of the waves and his flippers would become wings and he would be airborne.

He rose forty feet in the air − almost to the height of the mast, Bob thought. He was so close that Bob could see his eye, could see the rough folds in his skin, could see the barnacles under his jaw. The spectacle was so overpowering that time seemed to stop. Slade cowered in terror as the enormous animal, all twenty-five tons of him, fell sideways, slipping back into the depths and creating a wave so large it slapped the side of the *Santa María* like a thunderbolt. Slade and Russell skidded laterally as the deck tilted ever more sharply.

And then the boom swung.

As the boat came about, the wind caught the mainsail from a different direction, and the horizontal spar that kept the sail taut swung from one side to the other, gathering speed as it moved. It caught Slade and Russell on the side, and with the cant of the deck, the two had no chance. In an instant they were swept overboard.

Two of the capybaras slipped and slid to port and went overboard as well. The other two looked on in interest at their fellows in the water, and then, of one accord, decided to join them. Soon they had leapt into the Pacific and instinctively all four of them placidly headed toward shore.

Capybaras, Bob saw, knew how to swim very, very well. Under the water, their legs were churning, but their four gentle brown-furred black-nosed heads sailed serenely above the waves as, in the distance, Santa Catalina Island beckoned.

"Well," their expressions seemed to be saying, "this is a bit of a surprise — not something we expected when we woke this morning, but so far so good." They were adaptable and accepting, Bob thought.

Not so Russell and Slade. They yelled and cursed and slapped the water with their hands. Periodically they went under and came up streaming water from their hair and spouting it into the air. They thrashed and gulped and swore.

"Help!" Russell yelled. "Rescue us!"

Bob thought that was the least he could do. From a locker on deck, he grabbed a life buoy and two inflatable lifejackets and threw them to the two men. He watched as they struggled into the lifejackets, pulled the cords, then popped halfway out of the water so they looked like floating dolls holding onto the white ring.

José, at the wheel, was shouting too, and though it was hard to tell what he was saying, the tone it conveyed was shock and joy. There had been the astonishment and even terror of the humpback whale breaching so close. Had he been much closer, he might have hit the gunwales of the *Santa María* when he fell, smashing them to bits. A swinging boom was any sailor's nightmare, and although it had swept Russell and Slade overboard, it had not made José happy. But his tormentors were in the drink!

Bob stared in the direction of the island

where he could see a boat he knew must be the *Rainbow Bridge* in hot pursuit of them. Good, Bob thought. He'd hail Jupiter on his walkie-talkie and ask him to pick up the two water-logged miscreants.

As for the capybaras, Bob wasn't sure how he and the others would get them back onto the deck of the *Santa María*, but since there seemed no easy way to pull them from the water, he assumed it would be best to let them swim ashore and check in with them after they arrived there. They were docile creatures, and he didn't think they'd be much trouble. When José had first let them out on deck, they'd looked up at him, and then at Pete and Bob, with open-hearted expressions full of trust. It seemed to Bob they had this whole living thing all figured out. It was too bad, he thought, they couldn't teach the secret to human beings.

16

An Existential Envoy

It was four days later and Pete was back in Rocky Beach, together with Bob, Jupiter, and Mallory – and at the moment, the three boys were at the Evergreen Retirement Community, loading and organizing boxes in the living room of Walter Tate's apartment.

Today was the day Wally was moving in with Isabella Chang, and The Three Investigators were helping him do it, with the further help of Worthington and Rafael. Worthington had driven the boys over from the Salvage Yard in the Flex, and between Rafael's truck and The Three Investigators' station wagon, they'd be able to transport everything Wally wanted to take with him today in a single trip. The furniture he'd be bringing – his bookcase, his favorite chair and his desk – would be moved later on. For now, he was traveling light. It was time, he'd said, to let go of his old life and start a new one.

At the moment, Rafael and Worthington were outside with the Flex and Rafael's painted truck, while Bob, Pete, and Jupiter were taking a break from packing. The three of them and Wally sat in the apartment's living room drinking sodas – and in Wally's case, a cup of coffee – and filling Wally in on everything that had happened.

Now, Wally asked, "How did my delinquent son act after Rafael fished him and Slade out of the Pacific Ocean?"

"He was cold and wet," Pete said, "and pretty tired. He just did what Rafael told him to do and went to sit in the bow of Rafael's boat. So did Slade."

"Leave it to Rafael to show mercy," Wally said. "I'd have let them marinate in the brine for a while. And then you all went capybara-chasing?"

"That's right," Bob said. "José sailed the *Santa María* back to Santa Catalina and Rafael followed on the *Rainbow Bridge*. After José secured his sails and dropped anchor, Pete and José and I lowered the four capybara kennels into Rafael's boat, then got on board ourselves."

"Rafael managed to bring the boat close enough to land to unfold his flexible gangplank," Jupiter said, "and while he and I guarded Slade and Russell, Pete, Bob, Mallory, and José went ashore with kennels."

"By that time, the capybaras had scooted up a nearby hill," Pete said. "But they'd stayed together and hadn't wandered, so they were easy to find, and as far as we could tell, they were happy to see us. Although they're semi-aquatic, I don't think they like salt water much!"

"So where are they now?" Wally asked.

"Back in Mexico, with José," Jupiter said. "Bill's Boat Service in Two Harbors was able to fill his empty fuel tank, and there seemed no reason not to let him take the young capybaras back to where they'd come from. José plans to take them back to his Colombian partner — the one he got them from in the first place — so that he can find homes for them in Texas or Pennsylvania. It took him a little while to understand that he was free to go."

"With the capybaras!" Pete said. "And Rafael gave Rojo back to him. He clearly remembered José, because he hopped right onto his shoulder and stayed there."

"I'm glad to hear that," Wally said. "Though I would have liked to meet a bird that made noises like a carillon."

"Rafael also had a great idea," Pete said. "With a boat as pretty as the *Santa María*, and a parrot as entertaining as Rojo — and with José being so good at sailing and cooking and stuff – Rafael thought he should consider taking American tourists on whale-watching expeditions!"

"That really *is* an excellent idea," Wally said. "But I thought José didn't speak English."

"He doesn't," said Bob. "But Rafael gave him his telephone number and said he'd try to find him an English tutor – or even a translator – through his Mexican connections."

Everyone stopped talking for a minute while they sipped their drinks.

Wally cleared his throat. "I have to admit, cynic that I am, that the three of you have given me renewed faith in the future. You seem to have found answers to every question. It's far too late now to make any difference, but still, I was vastly relieved when Jupiter explained to me what had really gone on with my thermostat."

He paused and took a deep breath. "As you can imagine, I was a bit steamed when I found out Russell was also borrowing against the value of my house – and even more steamed when I learned he was planning to use the money to smuggle animals. So why did the five of you decide to let him go? I'd have thought an elongated period of heel-cool-

ing would have done him and his criminal partner some good."

"Rafael thought turning them in would
do nothing," Jupiter said, "and we agreed.
Russell won't be importing illegal animals
again, and now that you've rescinded his
Power of Attorney, he won't be bothering you,
either."

"Did they thank you?" Wally asked.

"I wouldn't say they were grateful," Jupiter said. "But they were relieved."

"And," Bob added, "since Russell left his
jacket in the cabin when he came to get more
liquor, the cash he stole from you didn't go into
the sea with him and neither did my cellphone!
I guess the cash wouldn't have been hurt, but
my cellphone certainly would!

"Once we got back to Isla Vista, we all
got into Russell's panel truck and drove to the
warehouse where we surprised Jack Cutter,
taking care of the animals. Jupiter and Mallory
told him he had to stop smuggling, and that
the capybaras and macaws would have to go
to a rescue center until we could find them per-
manent homes."

"He was pretty O.K. with that," Pete
said, "so I called Mr. Munson at the Rocky
Beach Animal Rescue Center – I volunteer

there — and told him we didn't want to give the animals up, but it would be great if he could take temporary care of them while we sorted things out. He sent a Rescue Center truck to Isla Vista to collect them."

"Do you think I could go to the Rescue Center to see the capybaras?" Wally said. "Before the day Rafael showed up with three of them, I'd never even heard of the beasts, but I grew to be quite fond of them."

"Sure," Pete said. "Maybe we can go together the next time I work there."

"You could tell from their eyes they aren't exactly brilliant," Wally said, "but they certainly mean well."

"I know!" Pete said.

"Maybe the four at the Rescue Center could be given to the Texan who took mine," Wally said. "I have all his information somewhere. This time, they'd be a gift — which would fit in nicely with Rafael's rule."

"Well, I think we should finish packing the music equipment," Jupiter said, collecting the soda cans and taking them to the kitchen, then leading the way to the last of the open boxes.

Pete looked around the apartment. There hadn't been all that much stuff to begin

with, he thought, since most of Wally's be-
longings were still out at his house. Wally was
intent now on selling all the furnishings or giving them away and putting his house on the
market. His daughter in Sacramento would
help; he wasn't having anything more to do
with his son.

Pete thought back to the end of their adventure in Isla Vista. After Slade and Russell
had driven away from the warehouse for the
last time, Jack Cutter had volunteered to stay
and wait for the Rescue Center truck, while
Pete and the others walked back down to the
water and re-boarded the *Rainbow Bridge*. This
time, they'd had a very short journey — to Rafael's slip at his usual marina, where he'd gotten his truck and driven them back to his
house.

There, they'd showered, changed
clothes, and pitched their tents before sitting
down to a magnificent breakfast/lunch cooked
by Rafael's girlfriend Elena — who turned out
to be in her late thirties with short dark hair
and a merry face. She was clearly happy to see
Rafael when he pulled up in his battered yellow
truck, but she didn't seem all that curious
about what exactly had happened since she'd
seen him last. In this, she was very different

from Pete's mother – who would have had a million questions for his father in a similar circumstance, Pete thought. Elena's questions had all been directed to them.

After that, he, Bob, Jupiter, and Mallory had all gone to their tents to sleep, but that evening they'd had a cookout at a fire pit Rafael had built where they could look out over the Pacific. Pete had sat next to Rafael and asked him earnest questions about things like growing up and choosing what to do with your life. Even after his afternoon nap, Pete had still been very tired, and maybe that was why he didn't remember the conversation as clearly as he wished he could.

What he *did* remember was that Rafael had seemed to understand when Pete had said he felt sorry for Russell and Slade. He'd said something about the fact that when Slade was tying him up, he'd started thinking about what it really meant to be free. If you were a human being and not another kind of animal, then being free to do what you wanted with your own hands wasn't enough; you also had to be free to do what you wanted with your own mind. Russell and Slade weren't free that way, he'd said – and in Russell's case, he didn't even seem to know it. That was true, Rafael had agreed – which had made Pete pretty happy.

As for Rafael, what had made *him* happy had been the fact that, when he had asked Jack Cutter if his son Gabriel had had anything to do with smuggling the hyacinth macaws up from the Pantanel, Cutter had looked at him with an expression of such astonishment that it had been clear even before he confirmed it that he had literally never heard of such a thing. Although, as of now, Rafael still didn't know where the hyacinth macaw feathers he had seen in Gabriel's room had come from, he no longer thought it was because Gabriel had been involved in smuggling.

"All right," said Jupiter. "Let's get these boxes closed." It didn't take much longer, and by the time Rafael and Worthington got back up to the apartment, everything was ready. It only took a few trips to the truck and the Flex to get the rest of Wally's stuff loaded.

When they got to Isabella Chang's house, Isabella was waiting for them. She met them at the door looking radiant and excited.

"Come in, come in!" she said. "Your timing is perfect, and I have very good news! We took our four hyacinth macaws to the Rescue Center yesterday afternoon, so we could clean the wing and get it ready, and a veterinarian at the Center examined all eight birds. It turns out that four of them are females and four of them are males!"

"The macaws are gone already?" Wally said. "Are you sure you want to trade four gorgeous blue birds for plain-jane me?"

"I most certainly do," Isabella said.

"What's the good news?" Bob asked.

"Since it would be too dangerous to the populations in the Pantanal to return these birds to the wild, Charlotte and I spent the morning on the telephone trying to line up new homes for them. We found four bird sanctuaries thrilled to have mating pairs, and Mr. Munson is going to make arrangements to fly the birds to their new homes as soon as possible."

"That *is* good news," Bob said.

"Yes," said Isabella. She looked at Wally, who suddenly seemed to Pete a bit gloomy.

"I'm happy for the birds, of course," he said, "but I'd have liked to see them again. I had so many birds for so long."

"We can see them when we visit the capybaras," Pete reassured him. He had a piece of news he thought would cheer Wally up. "And I talked to my mother about the lovebirds she bought me that day in Veronica's bird shop? We'd like to give them to you and Isabella. You'd be with them a whole lot more than I could be."

Wally's face lit up. "Really?" he said. "A pair of lovebirds?" He looked slyly at Isabella. "The three of you are a gift that just keeps giving."

Isabella laughed. "We'd love to have them," she said. "We'll put them in the living room, near the big glass doors to the garden."

When they finished unpacking the truck and the station wagon, Wally and Isabella came out to say goodbye.

"Thank you all so very much. While I can't really regret not having been with you on your adventure, I do wish I'd seen that whale breaching," Wally said.

"It was fantastic," Pete said. He turned to Rafael. "I've been meaning to tell you that the carving your friend did of the humpback really caught the spirit of that whale we saw."

"I'm glad you brought that up," Rafael said, "because I have the carving with me, and I want to give it back to the three of you. When we got back to my house the other day, Mallory mentioned to Elena that you've been collecting mementos of your cases. But I'd decided to give it to you, anyway, the moment I saw the whale breach and the wave tilt the *Santa María* sideways."

Rafael opened the truck cap, lifted out the carving, and set it in Pete's hands. To Jupiter, he said, "You're the one who gave me the carving to begin with, so I'm really just keeping the gift in motion. Still, it now belongs to the three of you together."

"Thanks!" Pete said. "This means a lot to us."

"It's not just a perfect memento, but a really fine carving," Jupiter said. "Your friend is an artist."

Rafael nodded. "He really is," he said.

Then he drove away while they all stood waving. After the boys had also said goodbye to Isabella and Wally, they piled into their car. Pete had to admit that, as much as he liked Mallory, he was glad to be back in his old seat, riding shotgun. Her mother had needed Mallory this morning at home. Back at the Salvage Yard, Worthington let the boys off and climbed into his Mini-Cooper. In Headquarters, Pete took his usual seat next to Bob, while Jupiter sat behind the desk. He reached out to where Pete had set the whale and picked it up.

"We've been quite lucky with the mementos we've been collecting, and this ranks with the best of them. How do you think we should display it?”

“Maybe put a picture hanger hook on the back of it?” Bob asked.

“I don’t know,” Jupiter said. “I wouldn’t want it to fall someday and break or crack.”

“Maybe we could build a little shelf for it,” Pete said, “with brackets. We could put a back on the shelf and paint both the back and the shelf blue, like the ocean.”

“That sounds like a great idea,” Jupiter said.

Pete looked around for space on the wall for a shelf.

“You know,” he said, “Mallory was right about this place. It *is* pretty crowded in here these days. We were all surprised when she brought it up, but she wasn’t wrong. We’ve been holding onto so much stuff we don’t even know what we have any more. Maybe we really should think about a new Headquarters.”

“I agree with you completely. We should,” Jupiter said inscrutably, and Pete was sure there was a fifty-fifty chance that Jupiter would forget the whole idea as quickly as possible.

Pete smiled to himself. “I forgot to tell you that I heard from Connor O’Malley the other night," he said. "Just after we got back from Isla Vista. He called me at home to say he was ready to send us our chimera stickers, and they're getting here today."

"But that's great!" Bob said. "Has UPS been here yet?"

"I don't think so," Jupiter said. "Did he get the stickers made in three different sizes, as we discussed?"

"I'm sure he did," Pete said. "All he mentioned was that they're very cool. He also said he was coming south for a conference for Four-H Club mentors before school starts and that he hoped he would get to see us. Anyway," he added. "I'm glad I remembered before UPS actually got here."

"You know," Bob said, "it's hard to believe, but it was two cases ago, before this case filled with animals, that Pete had the idea for the three of us as a chimera."

"It's a good thing, too," Jupiter said, "because I think the chimera's going to be far more convincing as a golden eagle, a bobcat, and a bighorn sheep than if it had been a macaw, a capybara, and a humpback whale."

"Good going, Pete!" Bob said. "I can't wait to see the stickers."

To tell the truth, Pete couldn't either,

and it felt good to have his friends congratulate him again on his idea.

Jupiter cleared his throat and turned to Bob.

"I assume that any day now you'll be writing up your notes for our website," he said. "I hope you have as good a memory as I think you have, because there was a long time there when you can't have been taking very many notes."

Bob smiled. "No," he said. "You're right. But I think I remember everything important."

"Have you thought of a title yet?" Pete asked.

"No," Bob said. "I really haven't. Except that we're up to 'E,' and I've been thinking that maybe I could use 'existential' for the adjective. Ever since I heard that Slade and Russell's band was called Existential Evil, I've had the word 'existential' in my head."

"I have, too!" said Pete. "Although I've had the word "evil" in it, too. We actually don't run into that on our cases all that often — though since I can't really define it, I don't even know how I know!"

Bob and Jupiter both smiled, and Bob said, "I think it's one of those things where you know it when you see it."

"I guess," said Pete. "Though I hope I figure out what it really *is*, one day. Anyway, when my mom took me to Veronica's bird shop we talked about what existential meant, and she said that existential questions were about how and whether life has meaning, and why we exist. She said she liked the word, because there aren't all that many words in English that remind you of how *interesting* existence really is. It is, too. There's nothing more interesting than life – at least for macaws and capybaras and humpback whales and sea otters."

Pete looked around Headquarters to find something other than the whale to try to illustrate what he meant.

"What's in that box in the corner?" he asked.

Without waiting for an answer, he got to his feet and went to inspect it. When he opened it, there, on top of a jumble of other stuff, were some old bicycle helmets.

"Look at this!" he said, pulling one out. He'd had it when he was eight, he thought, and it was a beauty. It was styled like the head of a shark – a sloped green dome with malevolent yellow eyes, a painted row of glittering sharp white teeth, and a fin sticking from the back. His mother had tried to throw it out or give it away, but he had rescued it and brought it to the Salvage Yard. Instinctively he tried to put it on and found it was much too small for him.

"Your head's gotten too big," Bob said, laughing.

"Maybe they make a larger shark," Jupiter deadpanned.

"Remember that black and red Mohawk you used to have?" Bob asked. "The one with rubber bristles sticking straight up?"

"Pete has always had a taste for the wild and wacky," Jupiter observed. "Though that lime green shark may be the wildest of all."

"Well, anyway," Pete said to the others, "my mother also said that of course life has meaning, and that people exist to find it! The only thing is, what would the noun be if you used existential for the title?"

"I don't know," Bob said. "Last night I looked in my dictionary for nouns that started with 'e', and I found "eyrie" and "envoy" and "emissary" and "embargo" but I couldn't quite see how to use any of them in a title. The only thing I could think of was that I saw a shooting star out of the cabin window of José's boat, and that maybe you could say it was an envoy from the heavens. Or something like that."

"An envoy!" Pete almost shouted. "Like what Rafael is when he visits the schools! Except that he represents the Chumash, not the stars. But I actually don't think it *should* be a shooting star, anyway, because shooting stars aren't alive. The shooting star was nice, but the *real* envoy in this case has to be the humpback whale."

"I agree," said Jupiter. "That whale was really something."

He was going to say more about this, but just then the intercom squawked.

"Boys?" Aunt Mathilda's voice said. "Are you there? Billy just left a UPS package at the office. It's addressed to The Three Investigators."

In his haste to lead the way out of Headquarters, Pete almost tripped, but soon he and Bob and Jupiter were sitting on the porch of the office, tearing open a big flat box.

Inside were not three, but *four* sticker sizes. One set was big enough to replace the chimera sticker they'd bought with the Flex, and another set was small enough to adhere to their Three Investigators cards. The other two could be put on books or notebooks or electronic devices, and as Pete sat admiring the stickers – all in brilliant colors – he could hardly believe this chimera logo had been his idea.

Of course, there had been chimeras ever since the Greeks or whoever it was had dreamed them up. But even though the idea of a three-headed animal was an old one, he'd been the one who had seen how it applied to The Three Investigators, he who'd imagined Jupiter as a golden eagle and Bob a bobcat, and he who'd been able to see himself as a big-horn sheep. He was the one who had asked Connor O'Malley to take his idea and make it a reality.

Bob must have been thinking the same sort of thing just then, because he said, "This was such a great idea of yours, Pete. We'll have to pick a good time before school starts to scrape off the sticker that came with the Flex and put your chimera up instead."

At Bob's compliment – and for the first time since this case had started – Pete couldn't stop the blush that spread across his face. Luckily, it didn't last long, and soon the three of them were heading back to Headquarters to put the chimera stickers safely away.

It was awesome how well the three of them worked together, Pete thought. The case they'd just solved had shown that – but so had the way they'd come up with a title for it afterwards.

In a way, it was funny to think of a breaching whale as an envoy of – well, of what, exactly? Of the power and glory of creation, maybe – and of the way that people and all other animals shared it.

The weird thing was, just about *any* animal, on just about any day, could actually be an envoy in that way. With human beings, it wasn't that simple, Pete thought. No, a lot of human beings had very nasty traits – and all human beings had at least some of them. At the same time, it was hard to imagine any *particular* human being as an envoy – or a role model – for all people, everywhere. After all, people in different cultures admired different qualities of humanity in different degrees.

Still, there were some human traits – like courage and intelligence and enterprise and kindness – that seemed to be pretty universally admired, Pete thought, and if you wanted to live a life you could be proud of, it would probably be a good idea to find role models – or existential envoys! – who had those qualities, so you could see in action what they really looked like.

The fact was, in every case The Three Investigators had ever tackled, they had run into people to emulate, and people to avoid like the plague. This case had been no exception, and while Pete sincerely hoped he would never see Slade DeMarco or Russell Tate again, he was glad to have Russell's father Wally and Wally's student Rafael Solares in his life. Slade DeMarco and Russell Tate were familiar types, but Wally and Rafael were men who were totally *themselves* – and that was what Pete wanted to be, too, when he grew up. What he would *do* with his life, he had no idea yet. But who he would *be* – well, *that* was beginning to come into focus.

He led the way into Headquarters, then set the box of chimera stickers on The Three Investigators' old familiar desk.

ABOUT THE AUTHORS

Elizabeth Arthur

Elizabeth was born on November 15, 1953 in New York City. She is the daughter of Robert Arthur, the creator of The Three Investigators series. She was educated at Concord Academy in Concord, Massachusetts, the University of Michigan in Ann Arbor, Michigan, Notre Dame University of Nelson, British Columbia, and the University of Victoria in Victoria, British Columbia.

Before she started working on the New Three Investigators series in December of 2018, Elizabeth spent most of her life writing for adults. *Island Sojourn* – a memoir about building a house on a wilderness island in northern Canada – was published in 1980 by Harper and Row. A second memoir, *Looking For The Klondike Stone,* was published by Knopf in 1992. She is also the author of the novels *Beyond the Mountain, Bad Guys, Binding Spell, Antarctic Navigation,* and *Bring Deeps.*

Elizabeth's writing has received fellowships, grants, and awards from the Bread Loaf Writer's Conference, the Ossabaw Island Project, the Vermont Council on the Arts, and the Indiana Arts Commission. She twice received fellowships from the National Endowment for the Arts and was the first novelist ever given an Antarctic Artists and Writers Operational Support Grant from the National Science Foundation.

Her novel *Antarctic Navigation* was chosen by the New York *Times* as a Notable Book, received a Critics' Choice Award from the San Francisco *Review of Books*, and was chosen as a Best Book of 1995 by *A Common Reader*. In 1996 the novel received the Ohioana Book Award for Fiction from the Ohioana Library Association.

Elizabeth has also taught creative writing at Miami University in Oxford, Ohio; the University of Cincinnati; and Indiana University/Purdue University of Indianapolis, where she directed the creative writing program. She and Steven Bauer met in 1980 at the Bread Loaf Writer's Conference and have been married since June of 1982.

Steven Bauer

Steven was born on September 10, 1948 in Newark, New Jersey. He was educated at Hanover Park High School in East Hanover, New Jersey, Trinity College in Hartford, Connecticut, and the University of Massachusetts in Amherst, Massachusetts. In 1970 he received a B.A. with Honors in English from Trinity, and in 1975 he received an M.F.A. in English from the University of Massachusetts.

Steven is the author of three books for young people – *Satyrday*, 1980; *The Strange and Wonderful Tale of Robert McDoodle*, 1999; and *A Cat of a Different Color*, 2000. His book of poems *Daylight Savings* was published by Gibbs Smith in 1989 and won the Peregrine Smith Poetry Prize.

Steven's work has received fellowships from the Bread Loaf Writer's Conference and the Fine Arts Work Center in Provincetown, Massachusetts. In addition, he has been given grants and awards from the American Library Association, the Parents' Choice Foundation, the Ossabaw Island Project, the Massachusetts Arts Council, and the Indiana Arts Commission.

From 1979 to 1982, Steven taught literature and creative writing at Colby College in Waterville, Maine. From 1982 to 2009 he taught at Miami University in Oxford, Ohio where he directed the graduate and under-graduate creative writing programs. In 2010 he established Hollow Tree Literary Services, an independent editing business.

www.ingramcontent.com/pod-product-compliance
Lightning Source LLC
Chambersburg PA
CBHW021024310726
48969CB00006B/1528